This book is dedicated to the memory of
Belva Marie Gray

born: Orland, ME 1908
died: Cape Jellsion 2004

Chapter One

Ten-year-old Adele Susannah Abbott lived on Gray Island and spent many hours down on the shore watching and wondering about the world across Penobscot Bay. She watched the ships and boats coming up river on their way to Bowdenville and beyond. She watched the lighthouse on Jonas Point and strained her eyes to see if she could spy any activity at the sardine cannery. But, mostly, she stared at a white block that Momma told her was a grand house with white paint, a doctor's house with bedrooms upstairs and electricity in the walls so that a person could turn a knob and a light would appear on the ceiling. Pipes brought water into the house, and one could bathe and use the privy in a room specially built for that purpose. She couldn't fathom bathing in a room where someone had done their business, but she did not dwell on it; preferring to think about the many other details of the house. She wiled away the days of her youth trying to imagine how it would be to live in such a home.

Her small home was situated on the deep-water side of Gray Island. The town of Gray lay on the tidal basin side opposite Bowdenville. To get to town one had to take the county road, locally know as Hardscrabble Hill road.

There were no wealthy families on the island and it appeared that the further one traveled down the county road, the higher the poverty level grew. This phenomenon was so prevalent that locals referred to the extremely poor as *coming from the foot of Hardscrabble Hill* and, in the town of Gray, one who had gone from rags to riches had *climbed Hardscrabble Hill.*

The Abbott farm was not at the foot of the hill, but it wasn't far from it. It was left to Adele's Momma, who had never lived anywhere else. Her sister, Adele's Aunt Eileen, had married well. Immediately following the nuptials, she moved to town. Adele's Papa had not only come from the foot of the hill, but from the very tip of the toe. And when he married Adele's Momma, he had climbed up as far as he would ever make it. His wife lived in constant fear that he would one day drag her and their daughter back to the bottom.

Adele would come down to the shore to escape the angry discussions between her Papa and Momma. One day Papa found her there, as he also was seeking to escape.

"What are you staring at", he asked. The tone of his voice was more inquisition than inquisitive.

"See that white spot, Papa? It's a grand house with white paint and many rooms, one room just for bathing (she left out the other thing).

Someday I shall live in a house like that!" Her father struck her on the side of her head with his open hand

"Insolent child!" he accused and stormed off up the path. Adele quickly cupped her hand over her ear and bent at the waist until her chest was buried in her knees. She rocked back and forth, moaning at the end of each cycle.

"What did I say?" She cried out. But when she looked up, there was no one there to answer her.

In the weeks that followed Adele found more and more occasions to follow the path, now covered in snow, to the shore. The winds off the water kept the path partially clear, as though Mother Nature understood her need to escape. Every so often Adele would have to assist her, and she would sneak Papa's shovel out of the shed and laboriously clear the drifts. She was always careful to return it dry and at the exact spot and angle she found it lest she gave him reason to strike her again. While on the shore she would stare for long periods at the white house. The sardine cannery had closed for the winter, and the ice that formed in the bay prevented the smaller boats from using it. But if asked, she couldn't say when the factory closed for the season or when the traffic stopped, as her only concern was the white house.

In the spring of 1918, Adele sat at the kitchen table working on her alphabet sampler. She had completed the letter *G*, but had redone the *H* twice. The first try leaned in on both sides and looked more like her *A* and the second took on the appearance of a bucket. Her mind just wasn't on her needlework. Her father had left earlier that morning for town. He went to look for work. Adele was lying awake in her bed and heard Momma whisper to him, "…just do the best you can."

"Momma, Is it wrong that I should wish to live in the house", Adele asked. Momma was at the sink rolling dough onto a homemade breadboard getting ready to cut out biscuits. Folks at church said Momma made the best biscuits in town. Deep in thought, she didn't answer.

"Momma," Adele repeated, "Is it wrong….""?

"Goodness child," Momma snapped, "can't you see I'm busy?" Adele dropped her head and returned to her cross-stitching. Momma brushed the flour off her hands, wiped them on her apron, walked over and sat next to her daughter. She reached out and stroked the child's hair. "We all wish for a better life, child. But wishing won't make it come true. And it is wrong to spend all your time wishing, and neglecting the things you should be doing. …child that *H* looks like a bucket." Momma rose from her chair, untied and retied her apron, and returned to her biscuits.

Adele picked up her scissors, and removed the misshaped *H*. Pushing the thoughts of the white house out of her mind, she was able to stitch an acceptable one. She was working on her *I*, when the sound of a braying horse caught her attention. She dropped her needle craft on the table, ran over to the window, and peered out.

"It's Uncle Robert", she squealed. Her mother froze by the sink. "Momma, its Uncle Robert." Adele ran to the door and tore it open.

"Adele", Momma called. Adele turned her head to see Momma walking across the room, wiping her hands on her apron. She wore a pained look on her face.

"What is it, Momma?" She got no response. As Momma approached her, she took her right arm and swept Adele behind her. Adele followed her out onto the porch, as Uncle Robert was dismounting his wagon.

"Is she…" Momma asked? Robert shook his head as he tied his horse to the porch railing.

"No Peggy, but she's getting worse." He walked up the steps and hugged his sister-in-law. Then he reached into his coat pocket, and brought out a bag of candy. He bent down to Adele. "And how's my little pumpkin?"

"Fine! What's in the bag?"

"Adele", Momma scolded. Robert laughed. He handed the bag to his niece.

"Sweets for the sweet", he answered. "Now go find someplace to enjoy it while Momma and I talk." Adele sped off the porch and headed down the path to the shore.

"What do you say…?" Momma called.

"Thank you, Uncle Robert!"

"…And don't spoil your supper!" Momma shook her head.

When Adele was out of sight, Robert broke down in tears. His sister-in-law put her arm around him and escorted him inside. She sat him down at the table and said, "I'll heat up on some coffee." She stepped over to the stove, and took a match from the holder on the wall. She turned the knob to allow the gas to escape under the burner with one hand, and struck a match against the burner with the other. When the blue flame encircled it, she placed the pot containing that morning's coffee on top of it.

"I've got to take her over to Doc Pritchard's in Jonasport. She says she won't go unless you go with us."

Peggy took two cups off the kitchen shelf. She inspected them for cleanliness. Not satisfied with them, she wiped each one with her apron and sat them on the counter. She turned to Robert, and leaned against the stove.

"I don't think that will be possible", she began. "Stuart has gone to town to find some work. I don't know when he will be back…"

"Are you sure that he's in town looking for work." His distrust for the man came out in his voice. "I just came from there and I didn't see him. More likely he headed for the foot of the hill to find someone willing to share their liquor."

Peggy threw up her hand to stop him. "Now Robert, I'll not have you talking that way about my husband. He tries….but, he's just not a farmer." The hissing of the coffee stopped her defense of the man who never had taken his responsibilities seriously. She was well aware of the fact, but did not want to be reminded of it by her sister's well meaning husband. She turned off the burner, and poured coffee into the two cups. Her head was down when she carried them over and sat them on the table. She took a seat next to Robert. Robert took a sip of his coffee and let out a pleasant sigh.

"Peggy, you make the best coffee. And you're right. It's not my place to judge Stu. It is written; *Judge not, lest ye be judged.* I was just thinking that you could take Adele to the Stoners while we're gone. Leave a note for Stu unless he gets back before we do." He tiptoed around his true feelings. "And, if he can't find work, and we get back before him, then what's the harm?"

Peggy could think of some harm, but she felled to express it. "My place is here, Robert; not gallivanting over to Jonasport. Why does she need me to go?" Robert was bringing his cup up to his mouth. When his hand began to tremble, he steadied the cup with his other hand. He took a long sip and placed the cup onto table. He was still holding on to it, and Peggy could see the coffee rippling within the cup.

"She's got the consumption. She doesn't think that she'll come back home. She wants you to go so that she can say her goodbyes to you." He lifted the cup again. His hands shook so that the coffee spilled on them. He didn't seem to notice. Peggy placed her hands over his and lowered the cup to the table. She rose and wiped her brother-in-laws hands with her apron. He was weeping.

"I'll go", she conceded. "But I won't be dropping Adele off at the Stoners. Her Papa will be home, and he'll need his supper." She went over, opened the door, and called to Adele. She returned to Robert. "Now dry your tears. I don't want Adele to see you so upset."

When Adele entered the house, Robert had regained his composure. Adele went over and climbed up in his lap. "Thank you for the candy, Uncle Robert. I ate a few, but I'm saving the rest for later."

"That's a good girl", he told her. "Gluttony is one of the seven deadly sins."

"Adele", Momma started. "Your Aunt Eileen is very sick. Your Uncle Robert has to take her over to the doctor's house in Jonasport. He has asked me to go with him. His love for her is so great that he is terribly worried about her. He needs me to go so that he might gain strength from our mutual love for her. Do you understand?" Adele leap from Robert's lap.

"…My house, Momma. We're going to my house?"

"It is not your house, and you are not going. Your Papa will be home, and he will be hungry. I want you to make him a nice corn chowder. It will be the first time that you've had a chance to make one without me standing over your shoulder…."

"But momma, I want to go…."

11

"This is not about your wishes. This is about your Aunt Eileen. Did we not have a conversation earlier today about our wishes and our responsibilities?" Adele dropped her head.

"Yes Momma."

"Be careful with the knife, and be careful with the stove. If your Papa is not home before dark, make sure you light a lantern on the porch so your Uncle Robert and I can easily find the house. When I get home, I will tell you all about it."

"Okay Momma."

"Well, Robert", Peggy said. She had taken charge of the situation. "We have a long way to go."

It was dusk when Papa came home. Adele had made his supper, and it was simmering on the stove. She had gone to the outhouse, so he came into an empty house. He was leaning against the stove when she came through the door. Papa had the lid off the pot, checking it contents.

"Where's your momma", he asked her. The strong, sweet smell of his breath floated into her nostrils, and burned her eyes. She stepped back, and pointed to the pot.

"I made that chowder for you, Papa." He looked into the pot, and then back at his daughter.

"You made it." He seemed disturbed. "Why are you making my supper? Where's your momma? I done asked you that before. What are you hiding, girl?" Adele grew scared.

"I'm not hiding anything, Papa. Momma's gone to Jonasport with Uncle Robert." He tried to slam the lid down on the pot, but missed. It hit the floor and skated across it. Adele took two more steps backwards. The action seemed to anger him, and he took a step towards her. She cowered, and he paused. He turned his attention to the lid that was still spinning around on the floor. He started over to retrieve it, but lost his balance as he bent over, and toppled onto the floor. He seemed to find this humorous, as he broke out in haunting laughter. He drew his knees up and wrapped his arms around them. Adele was frozen where she stood when he fell. Her shoulders were drawn up by her neck, and she held her arms stiffly by her side.

"So, why have my wife and Mr. Wonderful gone to Jonasport?" He had stopped laughing and his brow was wrinkled. Adele blurted out her answer as fast as she could get it out of her mouth.

"Aunt Eileen is deathly sick and had to go to the doctor. Uncle Robert is worried as his love for her is so great, and Momma went with him so that their mutual love for Aunt Eileen will give him strength." Papa stared at her, and then shook his head. After two attempts, he rose to his feet and stumbled over to the stove. The lid was stilling lying on the floor. It had stopped spinning.

"So the old girl's on her way out, huh?" There was ice in his voice. He picked up the spoon that Adele had used to stir the chowder. He turned and pointed it at her. "Well, don't expect me to feel bad about it. That woman never like me; thought I wasn't good enough to marry her sister." He started to dip the spoon into the pot, but drew it up and pointed it at his daughter for the second time. "And doesn't that of husband of hers think he's somebody special? …Always coming around here, buying the two of you stuff that I can't afford." He moved the spoon back in the direction of the pot. Adele prayed that it would go in, and then in his mouth; thus silencing him.

13

She was disappointed. Another thought seemed to strike him, and he slung the spoon in her direction. He lost his grip on it, and it flew though the air. Adele ducked, and it struck the wall behind her. Papa didn't seem to notice that it was no longer in his hand. "What did he bring this time", he asked as he attempted to point the now missing spoon at her.

"He didn't bring me anything, Papa", she lied. He glared at her as he sized up her answer. Satisfied with it, he looked into the pot.

"Huh", he grunted. "Finally ran out of money, did he?" He dipped his fingers into the steaming chowder and quickly withdrew them. He shook his fingers, dipped them in a second time, and came up with a piece of potato. He popped it into his mouth. When the heat of it overtook him, he spat it into the sink. His pointed a red, accusing finger at Adele. "This is lousy!" Adele began to cry. "Stop it", he demanded. He turned and headed out the door.

Adele retrieved the lid and spoon from the floor. She cleaned the milky residue that was left on the floor and wall, and then retired to the bedroom. Lying in her bed, she thought of the white house. She longed for her momma to return; not only to hear the stories that she would bring, but to protect her from Papa. It was dark when she heard Papa throw open the door, and come into the house. She heard him stumbling, and a retching sound came out him. She left her bed and went to the door. He was vomiting into the sink.

"Papa", she called. "Are you alright?"

"I'm sick", he claimed. "I'm sick worried about your Momma." He stumbled past her and laid on his and Momma's bed. Adele stood in the doorway until she heard him snoring. It was so loud that it seemed to shake the room. She went into the other room and looked into the sink. It made her

14

gag, and she feared that she too might vomit. She lit a lantern, retrieved the water bucket, and went to the well. When she returned, she left the lantern on the porch so that Uncle Robert might see the house. Then she cleaned the remains of her Papa's job search from their sink. She did not want Momma to come home and find it. She did not want anything to distract Momma from telling her about the white house.

Someone was gently shaking her.

"Adele", whispered Momma. "Adele." She awoke with a gasp. Momma placed her hand over Adele's month, and whispered. "…Sh-h-h." She took the child by the hand and led her from the bedroom. The snoring she heard as she fell asleep had been replaced with a sorrowful moaning coming from her sleeping Papa. She could smell the corn chowder simmering on the stove. Her stomach was growling. "Have you eaten, child?"

"No, Momma." She used Papa's excuse. "I was too worried about you to eat." Momma took two bowls off the shelf and filled them with Adele's corn chowder. She extinguished the flame under the burner, brought their supper over to the table, and handed Adele a spoon. She sat by her daughter and tasted the child's first attempt at cooking without her supervision.

"M-m-m-m", she declared. "Adele, this is wonderful." It was the same chowder that her Papa said was lousy.

"Thank you, Momma. How is Aunt Eileen?" Momma reached out and stroked Adele's hair.

"She's not well." They ate in silence. When their meal was complete, Momma collected their dishes, and brought them to the sink. Although she desperately wanted to know, Adele did not ask about the house.

"I'm tired, Momma", she stated. "I'm going to bed." She rose from her chair.

"Sit down", Momma instructed. Adele complied, and Momma sat in the chair next to her.

"We had to take the ferry across the river; ten cents for each person."

"...Ten cents?"

"...Ten cents. It took us another hour to get to the house after we crossed the river. Well, child, I never saw anything like it. It had paint as white as a buck's tail; plaster on the inside walls. It's kind of a mud that hardens when it dries. But you didn't see it. All the walls were covered in beautiful paper with flowers on it, and men on horses in black caps and coats with dogs running along beside them were all over the parlor he used as his office."

"What's a 'parlor'?"

"It's a fancy room rich people use just to sit and visit."

"...Just to sit in!"

"Child, do you want me to tell this or not?"

"Yes, Momma," Adele pleaded.

"Well hold your tongue, then. Your Aunt Eileen was coughing and spitting up to beat the band, and Doctor Pritchard took her upstairs to a bedroom. Cherubs, little baby angels, were all over the walls and the Blessed Jesus hung at the head of the bed, just like down at the church, but smaller. So, Dr. Pritchard says to your Uncle Robert that she'd have to stay there awhile. He felt she was too sick to make the trip down to the county hospital. Well, your uncle Robert agreed because he was awful worried about her. As we were getting ready to go, I say to him to ask about the location of the privy, it being such a long trip back. Well, you know what, Doctor Pritchard's wife, who seemed to me to be lacking in the Christian charity you would expect in a doctor's wife, opens the door to a room and directs me into it. 'Be careful,' she says, like I was gonna break something. Well, this room had a washtub big enough for me and you both, and it was sitting up off the floor on eagle's claws, brass ones, not real ones. Next to it was a washbasin with a spigot on the wall above it to fill it from the pipes in the wall. And next to that was a commode. 'Pull that chain when you're done' she says to me, and leaves me there to do my business. Now you know your Momma ain't one to be afraid of trying new things, so I sit myself right down and did my business. And when I was done, I pulled that chain, and water came down from a pipe attached to the commode from a big square bucket above it and washed my waste right outta there. I had no idea where, but on the way back; your Uncle Robert tells me that that commode is connected to another pipe that sent that stuff to a stream out back and all the way to the Penobscot Bay." Momma rose from her chair and stretched. "I think I'll always feel a little guilty taking such wonder in a place that will surely claim my sister."

The next week Uncle Robert came by with one of Aunt Eileen's dresses. He told Momma that Eileen wanted her to have it. Momma wore it to her sister's funeral.

Chapter Two

Not long after Aunt Eileen was laid in her final resting place, Momma sent Papa to town to try, again, to find work. It took him five days to not find any. On the morning of his return, he stepped into the modest home to find his daughter sweeping the kitchen floor. His eyes were red and swollen, and he smelled something awful. Adele dropped her broom at the sight of him. She hurried forward, but stopped short of him when he belched. A foul odor rose around him.

"Papa, are you okay? Are you gonna be sick?" Momma came hurrying in from the bedroom where she had been washing the floor.

"Adele, take your book and go outside and read."

"Momma, I've read that book twice already, and…."

"Do as I say child!" Momma scolded. Adele dutifully went into the bedroom and got her dog-eared copy of *Heidi* and headed out the door. Papa never looked up at her and Momma was glaring at Papa. Adele headed down her path and turned back to see Momma peering out of the kitchen window, then letting the curtain drop, as she turned her attention to her husband.

When Adele got to the shore, she sat on her rock and looked across the bay.

"I guess that would be all right," she said to no one, "If it went all the way to the bay. A body wouldn't have to throw in lime and hold her nose in the summer heat, or freeze her backside off in the winter." That settled she went on to more pleasant visions when she heard heavy footsteps on the path. She knew them to be Papa's steps; Momma's were lighter. She quickly pulled her book out of the large pocket in the front of her dress and opened it to a page she was not reading. As an afterthought and an added measure of safety, she shifted her position on the rock to face the lighthouse.

"Oh Papa," she would say. "You gave me a start. I was so into my book." But she never had a chance to try out her excuse. The footsteps stopped halfway down the path. Then she heard them going away. She turned to see Papa, head down, hands stuffed into the pockets of his overalls. It was the image of her father she carried for the remainder of her life. It was the last time she ever saw him.

Things were different after Papa left. Momma hadn't told her that he wasn't coming back and Adele never questioned his absence. But Momma was different. Adele came up from the shore one day and found her in Aunt Eileen's dress.

"Just wanted to see if I could still get in it," Momma explained.

Supper one night consisted of boiled chicken and turnip greens. Adele wasn't too hungry and pushed the food with her fork in circles on the plate.

"You better eat that, child," Momma said between bites. "It may be the only chicken in our pot for some time to come." Then she laughed. But it was not Momma's laugh. It was different. And Momma quit making biscuits. They had to scrape the green off the last ones they ate. Momma said she had grown tired of making biscuits, but one day Adele peeked and discovered the flour bin was empty.

Adele pondered this on the shore. She was so deep in thought that she failed to notice the sardine boat passing by, closer to the shore than usual.

"Hey there, little lady!" She stood looking puzzled. "Yes, you sweetheart. Whatcha doing all alone out here?" It was a man about Papa's age, but dirtier, if that was possible. Hair covered his face and ears. "Wanna go for a boat ride?" A man next to him, as equally dirty and hairy, slapped him on the back and both laughed. Adele turned and bolted up the path. Behind her she heard more laughter and the chugging of the boat continuing up the river.

She didn't tell Momma about the men and she didn't go to the shore after that. When she felt the need to see the house, she would be content to go halfway down the path to the spot she last saw Papa. The house was smaller and harder to make out from that vantage point, but she knew it was there.

Spring had come to Maine and on one morning Adele woke up to the sound of water being poured into the washtub. She went into the kitchen and found Momma naked, standing in the tub. She was rinsing the soap off her body. "You're next, child."

"But Momma, it's only Wednesday."

"I know the day. Hurry before the water chills."

Momma came out of the bedroom just as Adele was toweling off. She had on Aunt Eileen's dress. "Put on your Sunday dress and get the good shoes your Uncle Robert sent you. Don't put them on. Carry them. We have to go to Bowdenville and they'll blister your feet on the walk. Dirty feet's better than blistered feet."

"Momma, why are we going to Bowdenville?"

"Momma needs to get a job. We're taking the ferry to Jonasport." Adele dashed into the bedroom in a flash, leaving Momma laughing at her sudden burst of speed. Adele returned near as quickly as she left, ready for the trip. "Do you think you can go all that way, Adele? It's a long walk up Hardscrabble Hill for a little girl."

"Yes, Momma, I'm not a little girl". She wanted to say that men were already hollering for her, but instead said, "I'd walk to the North Pole to see that house."

Momma was right. It was a long way to Bowdenville. But Adele didn't complain. She thanked the Lord for her Momma's wisdom in telling her not to wear her shoes. They had become like lead in her hands. She could imagine what they would have done to her feet. When the town came into view, she felt tremendous relief. They crossed the tidal basin; the water's doing their disappearing act into the middle of the ocean. And when they climbed up to the road, Momma pulled some leaves off a maple tree. She stepped into a mud puddle and washed her feet and used the leaves to dry them. Adele followed her mother into the puddle, but lingered there, the cool dirty water felt so good on her aching feet. "Don't dawdle, child. We've lots to do." Adele dried her feet with the leaves her Momma was holding out and put on her Sunday shoes.

Adele Susannah Abbott had only been to Bowdenville once before in her life. Papa had a misunderstanding about a lost cow and Momma had to come and explain things to the constable. Uncle Robert brought them in his carriage and they crossed over on the ferry by the Gray Island town hall. It didn't cost near as much as the one that crossed the river. The farmer's association paid most of it to help folks get their produce to market. The 'hoosegow' where they let Papa stay until Momma came to explain things was on the edge of town and there wasn't much to see. And when she did see something to see, Momma covered her eyes.

This time they went right into town. The things she saw overwhelmed her. There were houses, lots of houses, with the white paint Momma described. And grand houses they were, but not as grand as the doctor's house. There were stores with big glass windows and in them was everything in the world, more things maybe than in the Sears & Roebuck catalog that Aunt Eileen had sent to Momma to choose a wedding present. Momma chose a bone-handled paring knife, which Papa picked up at the post office. But these things were here, not on paper, and she could go into the stores and touch them if Momma wasn't dragging her along by the hand. Buggies without horses carried people down the street. And she saw lots of children. Some she recognized from Sunday school class on the island. But they didn't wave back when she waved. They were with other kids she didn't know and the ones she knew would turn to the ones she didn't and whisper and giggle. She was so involved in her exploration of this new world that she barely heard Momma when she sat her on a bench and said, "Sit here, child. Don't move and speak to no one."

When she awoke from the spell the town had cast on her, she didn't see Momma. She stood quickly and looked around. Seconds before panic would grip her she saw Aunt Eileen's dress walking down by the docks. It turned and walked up to a man standing by a shed built over the water. He wore a black cap that was flat on the top and a black Sunday jacket over his overalls. Next to him, secured to the dock was the ferry. "The ferry," Adele said under her breath, "I'm really going to Jonasport!"

The man looked into Momma's palm and shook his head and turned to go back into his little house. Momma followed him, her arms waving in the air. The man stopped. Momma said something to him and pointed up the bank at Adele. He looked up, back to Momma, and back at a pitiful child waving at him from the park bench. He said something to Momma and Momma nodded. He said something else and Momma looked at her feet, then looked up at him and nodded again. The man then pointed down the wharf and when Momma started to walk away, he shook his head and went inside. Adele looked where the man pointed and almost swallowed her tongue. It was the sardine boat. She wanted to scream, to call to Momma, to warn her. But she didn't, she couldn't. Right before Momma got to the boat, she stopped. Adele was relieved, but her relief quickly vanished. Momma straightened her dress, and then tugged it up a little at her hips. She took the pins out of her hair and shook it down like she was going to bed. Then she walked funny, shaking her hips from side to side. She stopped at the sardine boat and put one foot on the gangplank that provide access to the craft. Adele was breathless as the dirty, hairy men came down the plank and surrounded Momma. Momma was poking their ribs with her finger and laughing like they were family.

"Momma" Adele whispered and sat heavily on the bench.

Momma was pinning up her hair when she came up the bank. "Are you hungry, child?" Adele wasn't.

"Yes, Momma." She followed her Momma into a store that sold food you ate right there. Adele would have been amazed if she hadn't been in shock by what her mother had done. She and Momma sat, and Momma looked at a board on the wall with a list of food on it.

A man in a strange little white hat came up wiping a glass with a towel. "Whatta'll you have?" He asked. Momma chose two sandwiches off the board and asked for two glasses of water. "You got any money, lady?" Momma slapped some coins onto the table and glared at him. The man looked at the money, and satisfied went off to make the sandwiches. Neither spoke until their food arrived. As they began to eat Momma told her sullen daughter, "Hurry up and eat, tides coming."

Adele didn't pay attention to how much money Momma slapped on the table that day. But she knew it wasn't twenty cents.

The tide had caught them and they had to wade across, their dresses getting wet and clinging to them as they walked down the county road to their house. They were both exhausted from the trip and went straight to bed. Adele had a fitful sleep. Momma had told her that she had gotten a job at the sardine factory and they would be moving to Jonasport. The dream Adele had all her live was coming true. Yet, now it seemed more like a nightmare.

The next morning came a little later than usual on the Abbott farm. Mother and daughter were both worn from the previous day's adventure and long walk home. It was well past daybreak when Adele woke to the sound of water being poured into the washtub again. Drowsy, she walked into the kitchen and, again, found her mother naked, rinsing off in the tub. "You're next" she said for the second time in as many days. She went on to explain to the young girl with the puzzled look on her face that city dirt was different than country dirt and needed to be removed with more frequency. Adele didn't argue because she felt dirty. She secretly hoped she could wash away the dirt of what she witnessed out of her eyes and the sick feeling out of her heart.

When she completed her bath, she went into the bedroom to dress. She returned to find that Momma, still naked, had rinsed Aunt Eileen's dress out in the tub and was hanging it over the cook stove to dry. "Adele," her mother said as she rubbed the wrinkles out between her hands. "When we were in town, I ran into Mrs. Stoner. She reminded me that your Papa had borrowed a crosscut saw from her Samuel and never returned it; big surprise. It's in the shed. I'd like you to get it and take it to the Stoners. You know it's only about a hop, skip and a jump up the road. I'd do it myself, but Mr. Tibias Anderson is calling on me this morning to make preparations for our trip over to Jonasport."

Adele was with Momma all day on the day before except when she went down to the docks, and knew she never saw Mrs. Stoner. "I don't wanna go to Jonasport," she quietly stated.

"Don't wanna go," Momma said in disbelief. "Child, you've set on that shore for three years I know of daydreaming about it and now that it's happening, you decide you don't wanna go?"

"But this is our home!"

Momma knelt by her daughter to get eye to eye. "Adele, we have no money. The garden is gone and the pantry is empty. The last chicken we had is in our bellies, so they'll be no more eggs. Winter will be here quicker than you imagine and if we stay here, we'll starve to death. The sardine factory is our chance. Mr. Tibias Anderson is an important man there and assures me he can get me a job and a place for us to live. It's my last chance to make a life for you and me. I know it's not as good as arriving by ferry in a horseless carriage, but it's the only way I can do it. I'm not the Lord Jesus; I can't very well walk across the water with you on my shoulders. Don't you understand?"

Adele didn't understand. "But what if Papa comes home? He won't know where to find us?"

Momma suddenly stood up. "HE'S NOT COMING HOME," she screamed louder than anything Adele ever heard. She bent her head backwards and placed her hands on the side of her head, elbows pointing forward and up. Slowly she lowered her hands and glared down at Adele, not noticing the urine gathering on the floor by her young feet. "Your Papa is a drunkard! He took a good farm and turned it into a wasteland. He struck me in the rages of alcohol and neglected his responsibilities and he neglected you even when he was sober. Now we're going to Jonasport, and if you like this place so much, you can pick out a spot on the shore over there and spend the rest of your life staring over here! Now get your young backside to the Stoner's before I take a switch to you!"

Adele ran from the house into the shed. She grabbed the saw and tore off to the road. She stopped and looked back, then grudgingly started up the dirt road to the Stoner farm. She knew her mother was lying about seeing Mrs. Stoner yesterday, and knew as well that her life would never be the same.

Tibias Anderson rowed his dinghy to the spot where he saw the young girl the day before. As he rowed he sang a little ditty. "Didn't get the daughter, but I'm gonna get the mother." He smiled as he sang it, pleased with his lyrical talent. He moored his boat and started up the path. His appearance had changed since Adele saw him on the boat and wrapped around her mother on the wharf. He wore green cotton slacks and an almost white undershirt. His hair was slicked back with hair tonic and he had drenched himself in after-shave lotion, although he had not shaved. It was a wonder Adele had not smelled him hiding on the path as she bolted from the house.

"Well, it's about time," he complained, peeking out from behind the tree he was using for cover. He was humming his little ditty as he proceeded up the path to the house. He didn't knock, knowing the coast was clear, and when he opened the door the first thing he saw was the dress he remembered her being in yesterday, hanging over the cook stove. She didn't bother to put it on. She saw no reason.

On the trip back from the Stoners, Adele did some thinking. Mrs. Stoner had confirmed that she had not seen Mrs. Abbott yesterday. As a matter of fact, she hadn't seen her in a month of Sundays. When Adele asked her why her Momma would lie about such a thing, Mrs. Stoner suggested that it *was* her Samuel's saw and maybe that her Momma felt it should be returned. "A woman's conscience is oft stronger than her man's vices," she informed the child. Mrs. Stoner did a lot of talking and referred to her friend Mrs. Abbott as "that poor dear thing" more times than Adele could remember. Then she gave Adele molasses cookies and cow's milk. Properly nourished, Adele made the trip back home. When she went through the door she offered no more resistance and helped her Momma pack.

The next morning Mr. Tibias Anderson showed up with a dinghy and a flat bottom skiff. In the skiff they placed Adele's grandmother's bed and dresser, taking special care not to damage the wood frame mirror that always hung on the wall above it. They folded the mattress and stuffed in the middle in a vain attempt to keep it dry. Then they loaded two small wood crates. One contained their clothes, kitchenware, and linens and the pictures of her Momma's family (and one of Adele's father when he was in the army), her mother's family Bible, and the Sears & Roebuck catalog. Adele carried her copy of *Heidi* and her Primary Speller in the pocket of her dress. She refused to trust them to the care of strangers. Mr. Tibias Anderson loaded his passengers into the dingy and rowed them to the sardine boat, which was waiting out in the deep water. He tied both boats to the stern and climbed aboard. But when Mrs. Abbott started to climb aboard, he stopped her, saying that state law prevented passengers from riding in a commercial fishing boat. Halfway across the bay, Adele stopped looking back to the large rock where she had spent a good deal of her childhood, and turned to face the house she would one day own.

Chapter Three

Mrs. Abbott had begun to wonder just what Mr. Tibias Anderson was up to. She noticed the boat slow to a crawl before they were halfway across the bay. She saw him run to the bow and look at the sardine factory with a spyglass. Then, he ran to the stern and looked from there. After two trips from bow to stern and back, peering through the spyglass at each stop, he nodded to the stern man, and the boat lunged forward and proceeded at a normal speed to the dock. When they arrived and the crew secured the sardine boat, he ran to the stern, untied the dinghy and skiff and pulled them along the dock. One member of the crew jumped off the boat and disappeared up the ramp. He soon returned with a wagon and he and other crew members quickly unloaded the skiff and loaded the wagon, almost knocking mother and child overboard in the process. Anderson saved them and hurried them up the ramp to the factory. Mother and child, hand in hand, and being tugged along by their escort, looked up to see their belongings being hauled away. Mrs.

Abbott protested and when they reached the door to the building, Anderson released her hand, broke the grip she had on Adele, and took her aside, but not out of ear shot.

"Look, Peggy, I can't just march you right up to the boss's office with your stuff on his boat telling him, "Look here boss, my new girl is here to get a job." I'm an important man around here. I told you. Folks will talk: conflict of interest and all. Now here's the deal. You're a widow woman from Lubec. That way nobody will be trying to snoop around to get dirt on you to take to the boss. See? And you expect your furnishing will be here any day. See? In the meantime ol' Charlie there hides 'em in his barn for a couple of days so no suspicions will be 'roused. See? Then we bring 'em out like they just arrived in town and old man Sloop ain't none the wiser. Now don't that make sense? You don't need them fancy things here anyway. The cabins are provided."

Adele didn't trust this man and couldn't believe Momma did. They'd never see their things again. And she didn't like him calling her Peggy. Her name was Mrs. Abbott. But when Momma didn't protest, Adele decided it was best if she kept quiet for now. She'd talk to Momma later.

"Now remember," Anderson said. "You're a widow. Mr. Sloop won't hire no runaway wives." He went to open the door, but when Mrs. Abbott reached her hand out for Adele, he stopped. "Leave her here for now. And don't mention her unless you're asked. If he thinks you gotta kid, he won't want you."

Anderson's Mr. Sloop, or old man Sloop as he was called everywhere that he wasn't present, was a plump man and he had the same odor of fish that all the men around here had, but his wasn't as strong, as he bathed more often.

He was perched behind a large desk covered in papers, a green ledger opened to the middle, and cans of sardines. A calendar on the wall behind the desk sported a drawing of a woman in red swimming attire stretched out with her hands behind her head. She sported a red scarf that was pulled behind her ears and tied in the back. The opposite wall had a large window that allowed him to spy on the workers in the factory without leaving the comfort of his office. He was smoking a fat cigar and was writing in the ledger. He paid no attention to the people who just entered.

Anderson cleared his throat when Sloop failed to notice them. When this didn't catch his attention, Anderson looked nervously at the prospective employee and spoke. "Mr. Sloop, this here is…" Sloop waved a flabby arm in the air, made a few more scribbles, and dropped his pencil on the ledger.

"What is it, Tibias? Oh, who have you got here?"

Anderson spoke respectfully. "This here is Peggy Abbott. She's the new cutter I told you about."

Mr. Sloop lifted himself from his chair and came around eying the woman standing before him. He walked around her checking her out. Her took her hand and examined her palm, then released it. She absentmindedly closed her fingers into the palm and put her hands behind her back. The large man went over and looked through the window, then waved at someone who was looking back. As he stood with his back to them, Anderson slapped at her joined hands, a silent suggestion that she was looking guilty. She dropped her hands by her side. Mr. Sloop returned to his desk, flopped into the chair and stared up at the two. He was trying to size up the situation.

"She's no cutter. Where did you get her?"

"She just showed up and asked…" Mr. Sloop raised his hand to silence his foreman.

"Where you from girl?" He questioned Mrs. Abbott.

She tried to remember the name of the town she was told to say. "Lubec. I just moved down here with… I just moved down to get away from the cold".

"You don't have the dialect. You must've married into the area. You married?"

"My husband is dead," she stated plainly.

"Lubec, eh? So, I take it you're going to require lodging?" He leaned back in his chair; dropping ashes into his lap that he decided to leave there.

"Yes sir."

"Well, you've got manners. I'll give you that. Tibias get her a cabin. Get settled in Widow Abbott. We start at seven am., sharp."

"Yes sir, thank you." He waved his hand again, and picked up his pencil. As Anderson opened the door, Mr. Sloop called without looking up, "Tibias?" Anderson sent the widow Abbott out and shut the door. She ran over to tell Adele the good news. Mr. Sloop glanced up and then made another entry. "You bedding that woman?"

Anderson laughed and lied, "Mr. Sloop, I just met her!"

"Uh-huh. Bring me the tally for today's haul." Anderson exited thanking his luck that he hadn't asked if she had any children.

Life at the Jonas Sardine factory was strange at first. But after Momma got her furniture and they got settled in, Adele began to adjust. There were many cabins the company had built to house the migrant employees, and the one they put Adele and her Momma in had a window that directly faced her dream house. The cabin was like their home on Gray Island, which Adele for some reasons wasn't supposed to talk about. If anybody asked she was supposed to say they were from Lubec. And if anybody asked what it was like there, she was just supposed to say "cold all the time" and laugh. Momma called it a game. Adele knew it was just another lie. Momma was telling a lot of them now. There was no inside wall to separate the bedroom and kitchen. The cabin contained a small cook stove that would probably heat it well enough in the winter. But there was no need. The factory closed for the winter. Then the migrant workers would go south to find work in warmer climates. Those who didn't migrate went to the cities to find winter work and housing.

But as Adele had to adjust to her new life, Peggy liked hers from the first day. She made friends with the women who worked at the factory. She told Adele that her new friends knew how to enjoy life. And she kept a lot of time with the man she used to call Mr. Tibias Anderson and now called Ty. She tried to encourage Adele to call him Uncle Ty. Peggy spent her spare time in the other cabins laughing and talking with the other women. She went to town on the weekends and spent late nights at the house Uncle Ty lived in at the edge of the property. She told Adele he was showing her the ropes of the sardine business. Apparently, it had a lot of ropes.

Adele spent her time studying the house on the corner. It was grander than she imagined. There was a porch on the side of it, and she would often see the doctor come out and stand on it. He was forever wiping his hands on a white towel. And he had lots of visitors. People in motorcars, people in carriages, farmers in wagons, and people on foot were a constant parade to his door. On more than one occasion late at night she would see one of the women from the cabins going to the doctor's house. And sometimes women in cars would come by with men escorting them. Always the porch light would come on, and the doctor would come out on the porch and talk to them, before taking them inside. The women with the men were usually crying, but the women from the factory never did. And the women from the factory never stayed overnight as some of the women in cars would, being picked up by their men the next day or so.

Peggy ignored the happenings at Doctor Pritchard's house. Even looking at it reminded her of her sister and a life she left behind. Truth be told, looking at Adele had the same effect on her. She had taken on a new life and new habits. Her job at the factory was to snip the heads and tails off the sardines that rolled past her on a conveyor belt. Women down the line put them into cans, further down mustard sauce was added, and then further still the can was mechanically sealed. It wasn't hard work, but it was fast and tedious. During the first few weeks she would return to her cabin with her hands cut and bleeding. Uncle Ty would bring her spirits that she would drink to ease the pain. And long after her hands healed and toughened she continued to drink the spirits. One evening after visiting her women friends she came in with a magazine and another bottle of spirits. She was lying in bed reading and drinking when she burst into sudden laughter. She told Adele to get her the scissors and she cut a picture out of the magazine and tacked it to a stud on the wall. In doing so she cut her hand. But the spirits were working and she didn't notice. She just kept laughing, drinking and bleeding. After she went to bed, Adele studied the picture. It was a little girl standing next to a little boy. He was whispering in her ear. The caption below the picture read *A Dark Secret*. Adele didn't see what was so laughable about it.

Sometimes Uncle Ty would come by when Adele was alone. When he knocked on the door, Adele, knowing his knock, would crawl out the window and hide under the cabin. One day she was studying the picture Momma had tacked up, trying to figure out why Momma found it so funny, and Uncle Ty just opened the door. Adele slid under the bed before he noticed her and she watched his feet walk around the room. He opened and closed all the drawers in the dresser and then left. He later asked Adele where she went all the time as he had tried to come and visit her on numerous occasions, knowing how lonely she must be with no one to play with, and he never found her home. Adele didn't answer him, but Momma said, "She's probably keeping time with the good doctor." Momma and Uncle Ty laughed and drank some more spirits.

"Momma, what's the difference between the spirits you drink here and the liquor Papa drank at the farm?" The question was not meant to achieve enlightenment but to prick her mother's conscience. Peggy sprang from the bed and slapped her. "Does that mean there is no difference?" She slapped her again. Adele turned calmly and walked out of the cabin. Peggy took another drink.

Adele and Peggy settled into quiet existence in the small cabin. Neither was willing to initiate conversation, as they both knew an argument would follow. The move and the personality changes in the mother seemed to have a maturing effect on the daughter. She diligently kept the cabin clean and prepared the meals that she and her mother would usually eat in silence.

She even took to cleaning other cabins for spending money, which she never spent. She never went anywhere to spend it. Her leisure moments were spent by the window watching the activity of the house on the corner. Everyday a new feature caught her attention. There was a narrow trough on the edge of the roof that collected the rain and sent it out a pipe on the side of the house. This eliminated the curtain of water that a person had to run through to get indoors like she did at the cabin and her house on Gray Island. She counted twelve windows on the two sides of the house she could see. The back door had glass panes in it and there were small slender windows on either side of the front door. Adele imagined the inside of the house must be as bright as the outdoors.

One evening she had pulled a chair up to the window in preparation for the evening's viewing. She had supper on the table and deduced that she had a good ten minutes of window setting before Momma came home. When the ten minutes turned into an hour, she turned and looked at the door hoping to will her mother through it. It was not the first time she would be left alone all night. She was pretty sure it would not be the last. She let out an exhausted sigh, arose and went to the table. She dumped the food off the dishes into the waste can and washed them. Then she returned to her viewing chair.

Just as she sat down, a face appeared in the window. It was a man's face. Adele screamed and fell backwards, toppling the chair. She scurried to the wall under the window and hid. She heard tapping on the window.

"Beulah," a raspy voice called out. "Beulah!" Tapping fingers struck the window. Adele froze. After a few minutes that seemed much longer, the man called one more time. "Dammit Beulah!" He slammed his hand against the window, breaking the glass. Her voice was frozen, but she found her legs and crawled frantically across the floor and under the bed. She heard the window open and the sounds of a man straining to get in through. She cried silently. A thud sounded and heavy footsteps got closer. Suddenly a hand grabbed her ankle and pulled her out from under the bed. Adele began to scream loudly and without inhibition. The man panicked and let go of her. She returned to the misplaced security of the floor under the bed.

"You're not Beulah," the confused man said. "You're just a kid."

The cabin door burst opened and three women ran into the room. "Get out of here, you bastard," the spokeswoman demanded.

"I'm sorry. I thought she was Beulah."

"Beulah don't live here no more. And she's just a child. Get out!" The dejected man started to make his exit.

"So what are you ladies doing tonight?"

"Out," repeated the spokeswoman. The two other women physically escorted him out the door. When all was quiet, Adele's protector called to her. "Come on out. He's gone." Adele emerged from her hideout, peering around as she did.

"What did he want?" The frightened girl asked. She was shaking furiously. The woman set on the bed and pulled Adele next to her, wrapping her arms around the terrified child.

"Hell, girl, he wanted you. Well, he wanted Beulah, but she ain't here no more, so he figured you'd do."

"Who's Beulah?"

"Oh she's some old whore that use to have this cabin". She paused, stood up and shook her head. "But I guess we're all whores here. Some of us are just whoring ourselves to the sardine factory for a lot less money than old Beulah took in. But, I've had enough. This is my last season. I've met me a young man with a home on the back Jonasport road. We're getting married and I'll never set foot in this hellhole again. If you was smart you'd get out too…while you still can." She opened the door to leave. "While you still can," she repeated and left the child alone in the cabin.

Three weeks before the close of the season, Tibias Anderson, formerly Uncle Ty, was caught fondling the daughter of his stern man. He was beaten by the man to near unconsciousness and run out of town. Adele wasn't sure what fondling was but she was glad he hadn't done it to her.

Before she got her job at the sardine factory, Peggy Abbott spent most of her time reading the bible and a few guilty moments looking at the Sears & Roebuck Catalog. After getting a job and a paycheck, she spent hours with the catalog and only used the bible to prop open the door to get a breeze in the cabin. Every week another package came in the mail, a new dress or pair of shoes, a new hairbrush or another bottle of perfume or bath salts. She didn't worry about saving for winter, because Ty had promised her that at the close of the season, she and Adele could move in with him. He wasn't supposed to keep women, but that fat fool would be going to his winter home and what he didn't know wouldn't hurt him. With Ty gone, so was their promise of winter housing. Peggy became depressed. She snapped at Adele whenever she spoke. Adele, having enough of it and completely losing respect for her Momma, replied with scorn and disrespect, and constantly insulted her and argued with her. One day after a long argument, Adele screamed at her

Momma, "Coming here was the worst thing that ever happened to us. I wish we were back on the island."

Momma agreed. That night after drinking an entire bottle of spirits, she walked out of the cabin and down to the shore. She stood gazing out over the waters. It came to her that, despite its hardships, her old life was better than her new one. Peggy Abbott desperately wanted that life back. Then, deciding that maybe she *was* Jesus, she tried to walk on water to her home across the shore.

Adele searched for her for two days. Rumors abounded that Peggy had abandoned her daughter and went to find Ty the pervert. On the third day of her disappearance the rumors stopped. The crew of the sardine boat found her body washed up on the beach below the lighthouse and carried it to Doctor Pritchard's house.

Chapter Four

Isabelle Pritchard did not enjoy the view of Penobscot Bay from her side porch, as her husband, Dr. Albert Pritchard, obviously did. He would spend hours rocking and staring off over the bay. Every time she attempted to do so, the sight of the fish cannery, that the locals seemed intent on calling the sardine factory, would draw her attention and spoil it for her. Immediately she would return indoors in disgust. And on the occasion when she would force herself to ignore the den of iniquity perched on the shore next to her lovely home, the wind would change and send a foul reminder of why she did not choose to share this pastime with her husband. She chose instead to spend her quiet moments with magazines to keep herself up to date on how the elite dressed and with catalogs to purchase the same or similar clothing. Or, she would lie on her bed and view slides on her projector of places she would rather be. She would look at one reel of Italy, then one of Paris, London, or the French Rivera.

However, she never left the viewings happy. Inevitably, she would end her session by throwing the projector on the floor in a fit of envy, induced rage and cursing her faith for making her the wife of a country doctor in a hovel of a town. It was not supposed to be this way. Her mother, a displaced member of Italian nobility, had implanted in Isabelle early on a belief that she was better than the common people she would meet in everyday life. Isabelle's father, Antonio Gongadella, was a banker and advisory to the royal family and of some minor noble ancestry of his own. Unfortunately, his salary did not match the expenses of his wife's lifestyle, and the result landed him in front of the magistrate for embezzlement and fraud. He was mercifully deported to the Americas partly out of respect for the man's family tree, but mostly because those he stole from did not want the authorities looking into their lives. Isabelle's father spent the remainder of his life as a mercantile clerk in Worcester, Massachusetts. He shortened the family name to *Gong* to better assimilate, or rather melt, into the American life. The decision had little effect except to further disgrace his wife. She spent the remainder of her life despising him and preparing her daughter to marry better than she did and return the family to nobility. She went to her grave believing that she had succeeded.

Isabelle met Albert when he was in he was still in medical school in Massachusetts. He had always told her that he planned to graduate and return to his birthplace in Maine to open a practice. She only half listened to him because she was confident that she would be able to steer him to a lucrative practice in Worcester where he would heal the wealthy and important people of her birthplace and she would attend important social functions and rule over those around her. She was wrong and reluctantly followed him to the coast of Maine some thirty odd years ago. Instead of living the life of prestige and social prominence, she was condemned to a life of medical servitude to people that more often than not she would not normally allow in her home. The years of stress and disappointment left her with crippling headaches that incapacitated her for days on end.

Today she was thanking the good Lord that her mother was not alive to witness what had become of her. She was completing the washing of the carcass of a drowned fishwife, and preparing the corpse for burial. She stripped the still-wet clothes off the body of the dead woman and dropped them in the trash receptacle. Dr. Pritchard had advised her that the woman's daughter would be bringing in the burial clothing. Isabelle washed the seaweed out of the corpse's hair and the salt water off of her body.   When she was through she followed her routine procedure. It was one that varied depending on the social standing of the deceased. After she bathed the corpse she would immediately go into the bathroom, disrobe, and bathe. Then she would don her prepared clothing. If the deceased were of some social standing she would dress in her finest arraignment and descend the stairs to announce to the grieving family that there beloved was ready for viewing. She would offer feigned sympathy and direct them upstairs. If the deceased was of no social significance she would don the uniform she choose to work in; an ankle length black dress with only enough white lace trim to distinguish if from a dress of mourning. She would call down the stairs for any possible mourners and stand at the top of the landing in judgment of the lowly people that climbed up past her.

Today she wore her black dress and when the little waif that past her went in to dress her mother, Isabelle Pritchard descended the stairs to join her husband and the men that had gathered in the parlor.

Peggy Abbott was laid in the room in which her sister had died. Her daughter arrived and clothed her in the dress Aunt Eileen had only worn once. The newer dresses and shoes were wrapped in brown paper with the new brushes and toiletries. Adele hadn't decided what she would do with them, but they wouldn't be used for her Momma's final departure. They were things that belonged to the new, unimproved Peggy Abbott. There weren't Mommas. She took one last look at the woman she lost that day on the wharf in Bowdenville and turned her attention to the baby angels on the wall and the blessed Savior hanging on the cross above the bed. Then she went into the hall and peeped into the other three rooms. One was full of boxes and some old furniture. The other two were bedrooms. She marveled at the fact that at the farm she slept in the room with her Papa and Momma, but over here even man and wife had separate rooms.

Downstairs Dr. and Mrs. Albert Pritchard, Jason Farnham, the High Sheriff of Soctomah County, and Andre Sloop, the owner of the Jonas Sardine Factory, were discussing the problem upstairs. Andre Sloop presented his case to the group.

"Look, I've got problems but this ain't one of them. I just lost my winter custodian and my best cutter is lying upstairs on your deathbed. The kid is somebody else burden, not mine. That damn Anderson, I'd never have hired her if I knew she had a kid. Jason, you know the state won't let me house other adults in a cabin with mother and child. I could've put two, three more workers in that cabin. I've got 'em stacked four of five high now. People are up my ass for that cabin. The kid's gotta go!"

"I'll ask you to watch your language in the presence of my wife, Mr. Sloop," the good doctor said.

"Begging your pardon ma'am."

"If you wish to beg a pardon, sir, I should think it would be for your vulgar tongue *and* your offensive smell," Mrs. Pritchard replied, holding her handkerchief daintily over her nose. "Can't you bathe prior to entering the homes of decent folk?"

"Please people" the sheriff injected. "We've more important fish to fry here than manners, if you'll pardon the pun". The doctor smiled. His wife and Mr. Sloop did not. "Sloop, I don't think your establishment is a fit place for mother and child, let alone a motherless child. I've had a man out there four times this month already. She'll have to go to the children's home in Augusta. The question is when. I've got two men overseas whupping the Kaiser, may God keep them safe."

Mrs. Pritchard and Mr. Sloop chimed, "Amen." The doctor abstained and his wife looked disturbed that she and this foul fat man shared even a common thought.

The sheriff continued, "I've lost one man to consumption and one went off to California to grow grapes. Grapes, can you believe it? Doc, you've got more bedrooms here than people sleeping in them…"

The doctor's wife interrupted him. "I'll not have the ignorant child of some fishwife…" WHOOSH! All heads turned to the noise upstairs.

"Well," laughed Dr. Pritchard, "I guess she's not so ignorant. She knows how to use the water closet."

45

"Two days," pleaded Sheriff Farnham, "three at the most". Dr. Pritchard nodded his head in the affirmative.

"Oh for the love of God," complained Mrs. Pritchard, and she exited upstairs to her bedroom to have headache.

After Sheriff Farnham and Andre Sloop left, Dr. Pritchard went upstairs to comfort the grieving girl before going in to check on his wife. He saw that the door to the patient room was closed and assumed the poor child was weeping by her mother's side. He started to open the door, but decided that his own angst must take precedence at that time. He went to his wife's bedroom.

But Adele was not upstairs. After admiring the claw-footed tub and using the water closet (she had no idea it would be so loud), she crept downstairs to see if she had drawn attention to herself. She listened from the foyer to their conversation and ducked into the next room when she heard Mrs. Pritchard coming. She was awed by the massive fireplace and walked in amazement into the next room where she found a large desk and bookcases that engulfed the walls. Each shelf was filled with books. There must have been hundreds and she thought of her two books hidden under her mattress at the cabin. Then she went through the door into the kitchen. Lost in the glory of what she was beholding, she almost walked right into the parlor where she would have been found out. She caught herself, placed her hand over her thumping heart, backed up to the kitchen wall and listened. When everyone left, she peeked around the corner and tiptoed behind the doctor as he left the room and climbed the stairs. She crouched at the bottom of the staircase and watched him through the upstairs railing as he started to open the door where

her mother lay. She tried to conjure up an excuse for why she wasn't in there.
But she didn't need one. He didn't go in, but stopped at the door, turned and
went into the room with the pretty furnishings that Adele assumed was his
wife's.

"He's going to comfort that old cold fish of a wife instead of
comforting a girl who just lost her mother. Some doctor," she snarled under
her breath. She was going to slip back upstairs when she heard something
outside and through the narrow foyer window saw a man coming up to the
house holding his arm which was wrapped with a blood soaked rag. "If I'm
gonna stay here longer than two days, I'd better make myself useful, starting
now," she thought. She went to the back door before the man could knock
and opened it as quietly as she could.

"Is the doctor in?"

"He's with a patient (not a lie, she thought). Come in."

She took him into the kitchen and turned the knob at the sink to
release the water. When it came out she jumped. She removed the rag he
wrapped his hand in and saw a cut on his forearm. She cleaned it with the
water and taking a clean towel from a stack of them in a basket on the
counter; she pressed it onto the cut and raised the man's arm over his head.
She knew what she was doing. Her Papa was a clumsy man and she and her
Momma were forever patching him up.

"Miss Abbott?" Dr. Pritchard called from upstairs. There was some
concern in his voice.

"In the kitchen, Doctor. We have a patient."

Dr. Pritchard came into the kitchen as Adele was lowering the arm
and lifting the towel to check the wound. "He's got a little bitty cut on his

47

arm," she said as a matter of fact. "It's a clean cut, no jagged edges. I think the bleeding has stopped." Dr. Pritchard took the patient into his parlor, which served as an office. He examined the wound, applied tincture of iodine to ward off infection, and followed with a bandage. The patient checked out the doctor's handiwork and commented, "Your daughter makes a pretty good little nurse," and patted Adele on the head.

"Oh," she replied, "I'm not his daughter. I'm his assistant." The man promised to pay the doctor later and left. Dr. Pritchard washed his hands in the kitchen, took a towel to dry them, and stepped out on the porch to finish the job.

"Wash your hands," he instructed as he left the kitchen. She obeyed and followed him out to the porch, towel in hand. He was sitting in a rocker when she came out. "So, assistant, you seem to know what you're doing."

She leaned against the railing facing him. "Yes, and I know what you do, too."

"Pardon?"

"I know what you do here," she said.

"And what is that?"

She leaned forward so as not to broadcast the secret. "You take babies out of ladies who don't want them."

"And where did you get this information?"

She pointed to her cabin at the sardine factory. "From that window. I sit there and watch the going ons over here all the time. I see people, women, coming here at night. And I get curious."

"Curiosity killed the cat," he quoted.

"I'm no cat. So, anyway, I get curious and I asked one of the ladies from the factory that I saw come here. And she told me. I know last month you did it three times, and one must've been bad, because she stayed overnight."

He looked up into the top of his head, retracing his steps last month. She was correct. "And you're telling me this and patching up my patients to get a job?"

"And a room," she added.

His first instinct was to slap her off the porch. He refrained. "I see. How old are you?"

"Sixteen," she lied.

"You look more like fourteen".

"Well, I'm fifteen, going on sixteen," she lied again.

"Do you believe in God?"

"I believe there is one, but He's never done me any favors."

"We call that agnostic. That's the school to which I belong." Now it was he who pointed to the sardine factory. "That place produces more illegitimate children than cans of sardines. I got sick of bringing babies into this world only to see them abandoned at the end of the season. So I started doing the procedure, just for the women down there. But, before I knew it they started showing up on my doorstep. Mrs. Pritchard is not only my wife, but also my nurse. She is a very religious woman and prays for my mortal soul daily. Every time the sheriff shows up, she's sure it's to haul me away. Nothing would delight her more than to get out of the business. Have you ever thought about becoming a nurse?"

"I think it would be fascinating."

"Uh-huh. Do you know what confidentiality means?"

Adele didn't. "Yes."

"What does it mean?" He knew she didn't.

She dropped her head. "I don't know."

"I didn't think so. It means what happens here stays here. You can't discuss any patients with anybody, from the procedure to a head cold. Can you do that?"

"The sheriff hasn't been here to get you, has he?"

"I'll take that as a yes. I'll pay you with room and board. You will study the books I give you, and you'll not drink liquors or bring boys into this house. Understand?"

"Yes, doctor."

"Then it's a done deal. We'll go pay respects to your mother and then we'll collect your things from that cesspool down the road." Upon rising he had an afterthought. "Superficial."

"What"? She asked.

"It's not a little bitty cut. It's a superficial wound." Adele stored that information away in her head.

When they went upstairs Mrs. Pritchard was still in her room having her headache. Dr. Pritchard glanced down the hall and tried to think of a good way to tell her that the girl was here to stay. He paid his respects to Adele's mother and left her to grieve. When Adele heard him knock on the door of his wife's room, she took her mother's cold hand. "Thank you, Momma," she whispered. "I'm home."

Chapter Five

Nurse in training Adele Susannah Abbott was good to her word. Alcohol and men would be no trouble as she blamed the combination of the two for the death of her Momma. The books might be a different story. But she tried with diligence to read the ones Dr. Pritchard assigned her. Mrs. Pritchard, to no one's surprise, was opposed to the arrangement. But she accepted it grudgingly when it dawned on her that in due time she would no longer have to participate in the procedure or any other aspects of nursing. She would finally have the opportunity to fulfill the social commitments expected of, or rather benefit from the social standing afforded to, the wife of a physician.

Dr. Pritchard enlisted the help of Abner Thomas, his livelong friend, to move the little girl from cabin to castle. Mr. Thomas and the Pritchard's hired man moved the boxes, trunks, and old furniture from the spare room to the attic. They carried Adele's grandmother's bedroom set and the child's meager belongings over from the sardine factory. Andre Sloop was happy to have his cabin back and Adele was happy to be done with him. She barely spoke to the men as they brought her furniture into her new bedroom, except to give instructions.

"Put it here. Move that there. No, to the left." They held and shifted the mirror left, right, up, and down until she was satisfied. After they left she saw they had hung it too far to the left despite her instructions. She shoved the dresser to the left with her backside until it was centered under the mirror. Then she took some polish and a rag she found in the pantry and polished the whole set to a fine sheen. Momma had let it lapse into such poor condition. She was admiring her room, hardly believing that she was the only person who would sleep in it when she was called to supper. They had a meal of ham and beans. It was a tasty, but quiet meal. The doctor was reading a medical book and his wife was glaring at Adele every time she looked up from her plate. Adele would have tried to ease the tension by telling Mrs. Pritchard that she liked the beans, but she knew someone else had cooked them. They had a lady who came in and cooked the meals, then went back to her own house. She seemed to be a real happy lady, though nervous about something.

After Adele had spent her first month in the house, everyone seemed more at ease. Everyone except Mrs. Pritchard, but she spent a lot of time in her room with a headache, so Adele didn't see her that much. But when she did, Mrs. Pritchard was rarely in good temper. And Dr. Pritchard tiptoed around his wife whenever she was downstairs. When she was upstairs, he checked on her a lot. Adele thought this strange, it being better to let sleeping dogs lie.

One day Adele had just started a book the doctor had given her to read. It was about the human body. She was trying to read it but wasn't doing a very good job when someone knocked on her door.

"Come in," she said politely.

Dr. Pritchard opened the door, but did not enter. Keeping his hand on the doorknob, he said, "Getting accustomed to your surroundings yet? Oh, studying are we? Good, that's good."

"Well, trying," she confessed. "But some of the words I don't understand."

He released the knob and entered her room. He saw the spine of the book she was trying to read. It was Gray's Anatomy. "Have you any formal education?"

"Momma taught me to read and write. I couldn't go to school on the island, because I had to help Papa on the farm." Adele had stopped telling the Lubec lie.

"And what books have you read?"

"The Bible, the Sears & Roebuck & Roebuck catalog, my Primary Speller and *Heidi*," she said pointing to her library neatly stacked on her dresser.

"*Heidi*," he laughed.

"Yes, but I read it four times."

"Well, dear, this is a little too advance for you". He took the book from her. "We'll have to start at the beginning. Supper will be ready soon."

"Baked beans?" She was hopeful.

"No," he said, "clam chowder."

The next Monday at the breakfast table Dr. Pritchard advised Adele that he had enrolled her in the public school. She wasn't too keen on the idea, but she realized that it was for the best. She had considered suggesting it herself, but couldn't quite bring herself to do it. A bus pulled up and stopped in front of the house and sounded its horn. Mrs. Pritchard entered the kitchen with a satchel, took a pail off the counter and shoved both into Adele's hands. The pail had food in it, and as Adele later discovered the satchel had paper, pencils, and a large eraser in it. "That's the bus. Go get on it. And, for the love of God, learn something. I can't wait forever for a replacement."

Adele went out to the street and stepped into her first motorcar. It was long with many rows of long seats on either side of it. Each row had a window for looking out, but no glass in the windows. Curtains were rolled to the top, their purpose becoming clear to her when the rain and winter months came. Many children occupied the many seats. They were very loud, but got very quiet when she got on and took a seat. She remembered the Sunday school classmates she saw on the day that she went to Bowdenville with her Momma. When the bus started moving, the other children got loud again. The school was a big brick building. Adele was a little scared when she first got there, but told herself it couldn't be any worse than the sardine factory.

Because of her alleged age, the teacher put Adele in with the older children. She soon began to doubt her decision. The child was woefully behind in her studies. "Why do they even have a school on that God-forsaken island?" She poised the question to the headmaster after Adele's first day. But the child studied hard. And she never participated in the shenanigans a lot of the other children did which accomplished nothing save aggravate their teacher and stunt their learning. Adele soon caught up and even surpassed the other students. When the other students ate their lunch and socialized, Adele studied. When the other students talked and giggled on the bus, Adele studied. And when the other students participated in the extra curricular activities that Dr. Pritchard insisted that she participate in, she sat outside on the steps of the school and studied.

At home she assisted the doctor and avoided his wife. She read the books he gave her and sneaked some he didn't from the shelves in his den and read them in her room at night. She studied the glass bottles that lined the cabinet in the parlor and looked them up in the doctor's Physician's Desk Reference to learn their composition and purpose.

By the end of the next year, she stepped off the bus for the last time. She walked proudly up to the house with a diploma from the Jonasport School gripped tightly in her hand. Dr. Pritchard tried to convince her to attend the graduation, but she declined. She didn't care much for the other students. The girls were only interested in dances at the community hall and roller-skating. The boys were only interested in baseball and girls. To attend a graduation with them would be a mockery of the hard work she put in to get her diploma, as they would get the same one by working hard to get out of work. But she didn't relay her opinion to the Pritchards. She told them, "Graduation is really for the parents. And I don't have any."

"Well, we're proud of you just the same," Dr. Pritchard offered.

Mrs. Pritchard perused the diploma, looking for signs of a forgery. She blurted out her opinion. "It's about time!" And dropping it to the table she stormed out of the room, and went upstairs. Adele picked up her diploma, rolled it up, and held it to her chest. She stepped across the room and eyed the path that Mrs. Pritchard had taken.

"…Why…?" She didn't know how to finish her question. Dr. Pritchard rose from his chair, walked over and put his hand on her shoulder.

"It's not you, child", he informed her. "It's just that…well, it's not you. That answer will have to suffice for now."

As studious as Adele was before she received her diploma, she was more so after. She devoured the periodicals Dr. Pritchard received in the mail and the books she sent away for from the advertisements contained within them. She read every newspaper article that came to her attention that reported about anything remotely related to health and healing.

She set about to put her knowledge to use. When she learned that the Yellow Fever that killed five thousand people in New Orleans and Memphis in the latter part of the last century was spread by mosquito bites, she drew the conclusion that the same carrier might spread other blood borne diseases. She set out on a campaign to promote the installation of window screening throughout the county. She followed that with a campaign to inoculate the children of the county against childhood diseases, making Soctomah County one of the first in the nation to attempt such an endeavor. She launched a campaign on a smaller scale to stop the availability of the procedure at the Pritchard practice. When young women showed up at the door late at night, it was Adele who went out to greet them. After she did her talking, most got in their cars and drove away. And soon they stopped coming. That left only the less-than-careful women of the sardine factory, but Adele decided that was a battle for another day. And, of course, she led the temperance movement to rid her community of the evil of alcoholic beverages. She was becoming renowned in Jonasport and beyond as a leader in preventive medicine. And

Dr. Pritchard was proud. He entered the kitchen one evening as she was washing one of her dresses that had gotten stained by the blood of an accident victim.

"What dress size are you?" He asked.

"Size eight in a ladies" she answered with forethought.

"But you have big feet. What are you in shoes, a ten?"

"No," she said, turning, "I'm a size eight there, too. Thank you. Why do you ask?"

"Mrs. Pritchard has some pretty nice things she doesn't wear anymore and she thought maybe you'd like to have them. But she's a little bigger than you."

"That's not true. If she saw me in one of her dresses she'd rip it off my body. And you know it."

"Yeah, she probably would. If was I who thought you might like them."

She returned to her scrubbing. "Well thank you very much for thinking about me," she said with an air of sarcasm.

"You're welcome very much," he replied, matching her air. And he returned to the den.

The following week Adele returned from the former livery stable that had been converted to a motor garage. She had gone there to change a bandage Dr. Pritchard had previously applied to the wrist of the mechanic, who burned it repairing the exhaust pipe of an engine.

"A package came for you," Dr. Pritchard said as she came into the house.

"Me?"

"You're Adele Abbott, aren't you?"

Adele opened the package and found a stack of white nurse's uniforms. Included in the box were a pair of white nurse's shoes and several pairs of white stockings. Atop the first dress lay what she first thought was a brooch, but turned out to be a silver watch with large numbers and a sweeping second hand just right for taking pulses and respiration.

"Dr. Pritchard!" She said in surprise.

"What? Shoe's too small. I said you had big feet."

To stop herself from bursting into tears, she threw her arms around him. "Thank you!"

"Take your hands off of my husband!" Hearing the commotion, Mrs. Pritchard had come downstairs and was eying daggers in Adele's direction.

"Now dear, she was only showing her appreciation for the uniforms," her husband assured her.

"I sure she was, Dr Pritchard! I can't for the life of me understand why you would waste our good money on her anyway!"

"We discussed this Mrs. Pritchard," he reminded her. "We have to keep up a certain appearance for the community." He knew that would shut her up.

She let out a low guttural growl and marched out of the room with her hands on her hips. Dr. Pritchard followed her, mimicking her march with his hands on his hips, stopping short at the door. Adele had to bite her tongue to keep from laughing.

The picture Adele first formed in her mind of the doctor when she watched from her window was that of an evil scientist with a sick laugh cutting the babies out of the bellies of screaming women. That canvas had been wiped clean and in its place a portrait was emerging of a kind and gentle man. He took great time with every patient as they described their suffering. He spoke in terms appropriate to the education level of his patient when he needed information, and listened intently when the patient needed to be heard. When he was confounded by a particular symptom he spent hours on the telephone conferring with his colleagues. He would be up late into the night poring over the books in the den, arising in the morning victorious and telling Adele to schedule an appointment with so and so.

And the depth of his knowledge and his power of deduction was matched only by the skill of his hands. Adele spent countless hours handing him sterilized instruments as he repaired the damage to the human body brought about by nature and machinery. And she spent equal time watching as those same hands turned a baby to provide it proper passage in its emergence into life.

And when she was not listening, helping, or handing, she was writing in the notebook she carried in the pocket of her dress. At night she went over her notes. And in this process she learned. And as she learned she practiced, and before she reached the age when most girls are looking for someone to marry, she was looking for someone to heal.

Adele grew proud of her profession and, as vain as she knew it was she grew proud of her uniform. She had already replaced some of them. A few received stains from the bodily fluids she encountered in her daily routine and one was rendered useless when she cut the bottom off of it to make an emergency bandage. She kept them washed and pressed. She purchased white shoe paste and polished her shoes nightly. In the morning after she dressed she inspected her uniform in the mirror, making sure her watch lay straight over her left breast pocket and that her stockings had no wrinkles. When she passed muster she went downstairs to start her workday.

After one such morning ritual, she came down to find Mrs. Pritchard in the parlor.

"Good morning, Mrs. Pritchard," she said. Mrs. Pritchard turned on her heels.

"There's a patient at the door, and at this hour of the morning, for the love of God. Let her in. It's your job."

"Yes Ma'am. I wasn't expecting anyone this morning".

"Well, perhaps Dr. Pritchard was. You don't run this place, you know. Not yet anyway." And with that she went back up to her room, bumping Adele to the side as she passed her. Adele went to the door and saw a well-groomed lady peering into the window and obviously listening.

"Good morning," said Adele after opening the door. "Please come in."

"She don't seem to take to you too much," the woman observed.

"She's been ill."

"Well, I'll tell you if I had a maid to do my cleaning and door greeting, I'd be a little nicer to her." She was trying to be kind. Dr. Pritchard let out a chuckle from behind them.

"Mrs. Alice Maloney, may I introduce you to Miss Adele Abbott, my nurse."

"Nurse, well I would think she could afford a visit to the beauty parlor! Child, you look more like a waitress or, well…. a maid." Now she wasn't being so kind. Adele timidly touched her hair. She never gave it much thought. She kept it clean for reasons of hygiene and she combed it thoroughly lest the lice that infested some of the homes she had to visit infiltrated hers. But, she never considered a hairstyle. She'd chop it off and be done with it, if it wasn't for her position. Short hair on a nurse would never be tolerated.

"Adele," explained the doctor. "Mrs. Maloney is our local beautician. She's somewhat of an authority on hair."

"Dr. Pritchard, I've asked you to call me Alice. Everyone does."

"All right, Alice," what brings you here today"

"I've got the trots!"

The following day a bell rang attached to a door that bore a sign that read *Alice's Style Emporium*. Alice was sitting in one of her two beauty thrones reading the latest copy of *Styles of the Stars*. She looked up over the magazine and said, "What took you so long?" And dropping her magazine into the next chair and rising, she added, "Sit here." Adele sat down. Alice started by taking Adele's chin in her hand and turned it from side to side. Then she stepped back and got a bird's eye view and said, "Uh-huh." She took Adele's hair down and wrapped a towel around her neck. She bent her back into a sink and poured water over her head. Then she poured a little liquid soap into her hand and started kneading and massaging her scalp. Adele noted how relaxing it was and started to relax herself. When Alice rinsed her hair she placed a towel on it and told Adele to dry it.

"What do you wash your hair with?" Alice asked.

"Soap," said Adele from under the towel. Alice dropped a container into her lap.

"From now on use this." Adele stopped rubbing and looked at the container and read the label.

"...Shampoo?"

"...Shampoo. Ladies wash their hair with shampoo. Soap is for feet and backsides. Hair is delicate."

Alice began to work her magic on Adele. She snipped broken ends, brushing, combing, twisting, dividing, pinning, and more brushing and combing. She worked like a surgeon. And when she was done, the instruction phase of the operation began. She advised Adele of the proper care and maintenance of hair, how to style it, how to pin it without having the pins show and, lastly, how to prepare it for bed. When she was through Adele admired her new hairstyle in the mirror, turning her head from side to side to get the full picture. Alice gave her a hand-held mirror so she could look at the back of it in the reflection on the mirror on the wall.

How's your diarrhea, Alice?" Alice gave her a puzzled look.

"My What..?"

"You know the trots."

"I don't have the tro…oh, yeah. All gone. That Dr. Pritchard's a miracle worker."

Out of the corner of her eye Adele saw three young women from the sardine factory walk by looking haggard and worn. She wheeled around and looked into the mirror and saw a professional woman looking back at her.

"Yes, he is, Alice," she affirmed. "Yes, he is."

Chapter Six

The spring of 1925 was a busy time for Dr. Albert Pritchard and his nurse. The long hard Maine winter had taken its toll on the children, the poor, and elderly of Soctomah County. So busy were the two that Albert had decided that the best course of action was to divide and conquer. Adele had taken to calling him Albert when Mrs. Pritchard wasn't within earshot. (Mrs. Pritchard referred to him either as Dr. Pritchard or 'the good doctor'. When she addressed him directly, it was always Dr. Pritchard.) To facilitate his goal Albert bought Adele a 1924 Ford Model T Coupe and instructed her in its operation.

Adele had become quite the nurse, and sometimes picked up on things that even the doctor overlooked. For example she noticed on how quickly the morphine would disappear from the vial in which it was stored.

She brought this to his attention while she was reordering the medical necessities that were kept in the stainless steel cabinet in the parlor.

"She needs it for her headaches," he explained and refused to discuss it further. Adele dropped the subject, partly because she had too many other patients to worry about and partly because she felt little sympathy for Mrs. Pritchard. The course of her relationship with the doctor's wife had been set. Adele saw no reason to alter the course.

When the last can of sardines rolled down the conveyor at the Jonas Sardine Factory, the town was divided in its reaction. Those who sought refuge there were devastated. Jobs were becoming scarce in Jonasport, and jobs for women were even scarcer. Most had to move on to Bangor or Brewer, leaving sad faces on the town's young men, but quiet relief in hearts of worried mothers. The more socially responsible expressed concern for the troubled women, but the silence of most of the community revealed a common desire to let the whole thing pass. When the salvage company came and hauled away all the equipment, Adele was elated. Not only would she not have to dispose of any more aborted fetuses, but also the reminder of an ugly chapter in her life had disappeared. And the women that worked there would just have to look after themselves.

Late one afternoon Sheriff Farnham pulled into the new driveway that Dr. Pritchard had made to accommodate the two cars. The new drive would allow either him of Adele to leave without the other having to move. He was more often that not, the one having to move.

Sheriff Farnham rolled down his window. "Good afternoon, nurse Abbott."

"Good afternoon Sheriff Farnham," she replied from the porch.

Noticing the doctor's car gone he asked anyway, "Is the doctor around?" Adele waved her open hand to the empty space that his car normally filled. Feeling a little foolish the sheriff continued, "Well you had better get out to the Avery place. Mrs. Avery has taken to her bed. Good day to you, ma'am," he said backing out of the drive.

"And to you," she returned.

Adele left a note for Albert, collected her bag making sure it contained everything she might need, and headed down the road to the Avery farm. The Averys had no car and therefore no place to park one. She left hers in the road and walked across the muddy yard to the house. Her white nursing shoes turned brown as she made her way. When she stepped up onto the porch a rotten board gave way and lodged her ankle in the hole. She freed herself and leaned on the railing to examine her torn white stocking, which slowly turned crimson. The railing also gave way and landed in the mud. It would have toppled her, but she saved herself with an awkward acrobatic maneuver that slammed her against the wall of the house. In her anger she swung open the screen door with much more force necessary to facilitate an entrance and it came off in her hand. The mere two screws holding the hinges in place sailed through the air. Neither the commotion of all this nor the string of curses that flew from her mouth failed to bring anyone to the door to greet her.

Upon entering the house Adele found a despondent Mr. Avery sitting at the table drinking a glass of whiskey. She took the glass from his hand and poured it back in the bottle. She replaced the cork and placed the bottle on a shelf over the sink.

"This is no time for liquor, Mr. Avery. I need you sober. How is she?"

"I just needed something to calm my nerves," he said, ashamed.

"I asked how she is. I didn't inquire…" An explosion of violent, wet coughing came from the back of the house. She followed the sound of sickness into the bedroom. A thin, frail woman, ten or more years the senior of her intoxicated husband lay on one of the three sheet less beds, not aware of Adele's presence. She was sweating profusely. Adele set her bag on a wooden crate that served as a nightstand. From it she removed a glass thermometer and lifting the patient's arm, placed it in the armpit and lowered the arm. She looked at the watch pinned to her dress and noted the time in her mind (6:51, remove it at 7:01). Had Mrs. Avery not been coughing, she would have placed it under her tongue. But she knew there would not be a three-minute interval between spells necessary to obtain an oral reading. There was another way that only required five minutes to register, but she left that thermometer at the house. It is normally only used on infants.

"Mr. Avery?" She called. And when she was not answered, "Mis-ter Av-er-ee!" He came sidling though the door. "Bring me some water from the well and some towels or rags, or whatever you can find that's clean." He slid back out. When he returned she looked at her watch. The thermometer required forty-five more seconds.. She did not want to attempt to cool her until she got an accurate reading. She told herself that it would probably be for documentation for the coroner, not assessment for the doctor. With this thought she pulled the notebook from the pocket of her dress. She looked at Mrs. Avery, observed and wrote. *Skin is pale and yellowish. Patient appears malnourished; breathing is rapid and shallow.* She recalled lifting her arm;

66

skin is hot to the touch. "Mrs. Avery," she called. "Mrs. Avery?" She took the blunt end of her pencil and pushed it into the patient's chest. The woman did not react. *Does not respond to verbal or pain stimuli.* She took the patient's wrist and looked at her watch, and then she watched the rise and falls of the woman's chest and, again, looked at her watch. She calculated in her head. She removed the thermometer and went to the window. Holding it up to the light, she looked at the point where the mercury had risen and noted the corresponding number. She wrote into her notebook, *104.2/102/28.*

She felt Mr. Avery standing behind her. "Heat some water on the stove."

"I don't have any kindling cut. I haven't had time to, 'cause…." She turned to him. Her look said more than any words could. He left the room and the house, and Adele heard the sound of an ax. Using her finger and thumb she lifted the sole rag he had delivered with the well water. After briefly trying to determine the original color and purpose of the greasy yellowed cloth, she dropped it to the floor. She kicked it from her personal space. She removed a dress hung off a rope tied across the corner of the room that served as a wardrobe. It looked vaguely familiar and as she viewed the others hung off the rope, she recognized them to be the ones her Momma had bought through the Sears & Roebuck Catalog. With the bandage scissors she pulled from her bag she made a small cut and ripped the dress in half with her hands; another cut and tear; another cut and tear. As if by instinct Mrs. Avery's eyes opened and she watched Adele through a fog. Adele made eight rags and placed them in the bucket of water. She took one and placed it on Mrs. Avery's forehead, one under each arm and a larger one between her legs. When the rags reached the temperature of the fevered body, she replaced them with the ones waiting in the bucket, returning the first ones to cool. After she repeated the process several times, Mrs. Avery began to rouse. Adele was putting a cool rag between the patient's legs when twisted fingers weakly clawed at her wrist. "I know you," Mrs. Avery croaked and released her grip from the exhaustion of the effort.

"Don't talk dear, you'll exert yourself," nurse Abbott instructed.

"I knew your mother," she mumbled with eyes closed. "She was a fool wasting her time on that pervert."

"Hush now."

Mrs. Avery opened her eyes. Her head trembled as she tried to raise it. Her strength failed her and she spat out a frustrated cry. With forced effort she turned her head towards Adele. "You think you're something… all dressed in white like an angel. You're just a fish wife… like the rest of us; fish wife in hiding." She tried to laugh and it brought on a fit of coughing. When the coughing didn't stop, Adele took a syringe and vial from her bag, and drew up a small dose of morphine. She put the syringe sideways in her mouth and grasping Mrs. Avery by her shoulder and backside rolled her forward. She held her in that position with one hand and injected the patient with the other. She rolled her back, changed the rags, and covered her with a dirty quilt. As Mrs. Avery calmed and began to slip off into a state of sedation, she whispered. "Those are my dresses."

When Adele came out of the room the water was steaming. Mr. Avery was sitting back at the table. "I've given her something to make her sleep. You should go see her before it takes affect." He complied. She mixed the hot water with enough cold to make it tolerable, took a cake of soap out of her bag, and washed her hands. She left the soap on back of the sink as a visual suggestion. As she was drying her hands she noticed the liquor bottle was still on the shelf. However, the label she saw when she put it there was now facing the wall. Mr. Avery returned from the bedroom carrying a picture.

"I'm writing a prescription for pills that will ease the coughing. Get it filled as quick as you can (she signed it Albert Pritchard M.D.). Dr. Pritchard will check on her tomorrow or the day after."

He held out the picture. "My wife wants you to have this." A little girl in a blue-green dress with a large pocket was standing by a little boy of similar age and height. His arm was wrapped around her neck, and he was whispering in her ear. The caption on the bottom read *A Dark Secret.* Adele could hear her Momma laughing at the picture. She took it without comment. She picked up her bag and headed to the door. She stopped and turned. "If you can stay sober tonight change those wet rags every fifteen minutes; if you can't stay sober stay out of the room. You'd probably drown her."

"Yes ma'am. Ma'am about those pills; I don't have the money..."

"Then sell that damn bottle," She yelled and marched out the door.

Her intentions were to throw the picture out of the window on the way home. She didn't want to not accept it unless Mrs. Avery happened to survive the night. She didn't want to give her the satisfaction of knowing she had gotten to her. But she didn't toss it out. When she got home Dr. Pritchard was sitting at the kitchen table. Adele came in and washed her hands again.

"So what's the verdict on Mrs. Avery?" He asked.

"Pneumonia, I think." She handed him her notebook turned to the needed page. "Her prognosis isn't good. I gave her drunkard husband a prescription he won't fill, and instructions he won't follow."

Albert read her assessment and handed the notebook back. "We do what we can. I'll check on her tomorrow."

"That's what I told them. I'm going to bed."

Seeing the picture he asked her, "Gift from a grateful patient?"

She shook her head. "No, it's a reminder from a ghost." Exhausted, she went upstairs to her room. She took the picture of her father from the wall. She removed it from the frame and slid it into the family Bible. She framed the picture Mrs. Avery gave her and returned the frame with its new contents to its original place on the wall. She stepped back and looked at it. Then she went into the next room and drew a bath.

Chapter Seven

In contrast to Adele's life, which had been falling into place, Mrs. Pritchard's life was falling apart. Her dreams of being a social leader in the town of Jonasport were not materializing. She had chances to make it happen. The Woman's Auxiliary had appointed her chair lady of the widows and orphans clothing drive. The new young minister of the 2nd Congregational Church offered her the leading role in that year's performance of the *Peabody Pew*. And the Daughters of the American Revolution had thrice tried to get her to join their beloved and much needed organization. It was, they believed, the responsibility of every mature and decent Christian woman to strive to keep afloat the grand old tradition of the DAR. It seemed to them that today's young ladies were more interested in what was happening in Paris, France then what occurred at the Battle of Concord.

But, alas, she always had to turn them down. These blessed headaches were going to be the death of her, she would tell them. If only the Lord Jehovah would see fit to lift the cross she had borne all these many years. Then she would be more than willing to come to the civic aid of her beloved community. Perhaps by next years drive (play or picnic) the good doctor would have finally found a cure, though his failure was not for the lack of trying, so great was his love for her. And thank you for coming. Goodbye.

After the first telling of this woeful tale the ladies would leave the Pritchard home feeling sorry for the poor dear soul, bless her heart. And they romanticized at the image of Dr. Pritchard busying himself in a laboratory in the bowels of his house searching for a cure. They pictured him combining different mixtures of chemicals, watching them foam over in theirs beakers and selfishly trying the concoctions on himself, somewhat of a human guinea pig. The ahs they emitted showed their appreciation of a love so strong. But as time passed and they heard this story ever more frequently, the seeds of suspicion were planted and had taken root. They began to wonder if Dr. Pritchard was looking for a cure at all. Perhaps he didn't even have a secret laboratory. Perhaps the good doctor knew something they didn't know. Perhaps Mrs. Pritchard had no ailment that required a new and earth-shattering cure. And eventually, the offers dwindled and finally ceased to occur.

The straw that broke the camels back came on the evening the Friends of Joshua Chamberlain came calling. Nurse Abbott greeted them at the door. She presented herself in her white nurse's uniform cleaned and starched to a crisp that would make the general envious. Her hair was neatly put up in a bun without a strand out of place and not one single pin showing. Of course, she wore no cap of a nursing school graduate, because as everyone knew, she received her training from Dr. Pritchard and in the homes of the lame and sick of Soctomah County. But this did not prevent the entire county of considering her the Florence Nightingale of Jonasport. No school in Boston, Massachusetts could turn out a finer nurse.

Mrs. Drucker, wife of John Drucker, known as Jack to his friends and enemies made the formal introductions. "Good evening, Nurse Abbott. Keeping you busy, are they?"

"Good evening Mrs. Drucker, Mrs. Thomas, Miss Jonas." Miss Jonas, at seventy-two years of age, had never married and was a descendent of Abraham Jonas, admiral of the high seas and founder of the town. "I'm not so busy that I can't take time out for the ladies of the Friends of Joshua Chamberlain."

"Then you're familiar with out little group?" Inquired Mrs. Thomas obviously pleased.

"And all the good work you do," Nurse Abbott responded. "I'll assume you're here to see the lady of the house?"

"If she's available…"

The usual excuse was offered. "Well, she went up to her room earlier with a headache. I'll see if she feels up to taking visitors. Please come in. The wind off the water would chill a body to the bone." She showed the ladies into the sitting room. "I've suggested to Dr. Pritchard that we plant some trees on the shoreline to block the wind. I don't know; maples or something."

"A sound idea," said Miss Jonas. "Why a damn fool would build a house so close to the water is beyond me. They say the sea captains needed to be close to the water. But in my day…."

"Please Miss Jonas," came a plea from the other two ladies. And the entire room enjoyed a laugh.

A door upstairs crept open. Out of it a shrill, angry voice erupted. "Who's down there? Adele, are you entertaining in my house?"

Adele turned her head upward and in the direction of the voice. "You have visitors, ma'am. The ladies from the Friends of Joshua Chamberlain have come calling."

"Whose friends...the what of who? Oh never you mind. I'll come downstairs and see for myself. You just wait until Dr. Pritchard hears of this!" Mrs. Thomas jumped in her seat when the door slammed

"Ladies," Adele, embarrassed, tried to pass off the outburst. "May I offer you some refreshments?"

"No dear, I'm sure you're busy," Mrs. Drucker said softly. "I foresee that we'll not be here long."

"Well, I do have some paperwork. If you ladies will excuse me…" Quietly she stepped into the den and closed the door.

Mrs. Pritchard stormed down the stairs and stood in the foyer. She threw a glance left into the parlor, and then right into the sitting room. Mrs. Drucker, sitting in a Queen Anne chair just inside the room started to rise, and fell back into it. Standing to her right was a woman who must have gained forty pounds since she saw her last. Her skin had turned a pale yellow and her eyes were red and swollen. They appeared to have fallen back into her skull. The dark circles under them made gave her the appearance of a raccoon, a rabid raccoon. Her hair had not been combed out today, or maybe even yesterday. She was in a flannel nightgown in need of a good washing, and she was barefoot. She came down from her bedroom knowing guests were in the house and she wore no robe, no slippers, no dignity, and no pride.

Mrs. Pritchard, finally coming to terms with the fact that she had guests in the house, tugged down on her nightgown and touched at her hair as she entered the room attempting to present a royal presence.

"You ladies will just have to forgive my appearance." She said sugar sweet. "You see, I've been ill. The doctor is…."

"Looking for a cure," suggested Mrs. Thomas.

"No," she said sharply. As quickly as her tone changed, it changed back. "The good doctor, I was saying, advised me to stay in bed today. But, I can't possibly do that. As you can see, if I did, this house would go to the dogs." To emphasize her point she called, "Adele! Adele! Where is that girl? I can't believe she left you sitting alone and didn't offer you any refreshments. Adele Abbott!"

"She offered refreshments. We declined her gracious offer," corrected Mrs. Thomas.

Mrs. Drucker decided it was time to get down to business. "Mrs. Pritchard, as you know we represent the Friends of Joshua Chamberlain."

"And you're looking for a contribution?" *Two can play at this game*, she thought and smiled inward.

"No ma'am," answered Mrs. Drucker. "Well, not of money, we were looking for a contribution of your time. But I can see that your health will not allow it. So we will wish you well and bid you adieu." For the second time that evening she attempted to rise, but for the second time she fell back in her chair. Mrs. Pritchard had raced back to the foyer door. She scanned the foyer, closed the door and threw her back against it as if the Huns were invading. She turned her ear to the door until she felt secure that the danger had past. Then she bent down to the Friends of Joshua Chamberlain like a schoolgirl with juicy gossip to share.

"You see ladies," she began, "my health is an ungodly burden on me. My dear husband, who loves me so, has tried and failed to discover a cure; a cure that would not only alleviate my suffering, but would write his name in the journals of medicine for the entire civilized world to appreciate. But he has been distracted from his task. I have succumbed to the truth that his failure leaves me in the hands of the Almighty. It is my cross to bear. Unbearable as it may be, I will bear the unbearable for that is my cross to bear, sayeth the Lord." She paced the room as she preached, walking in circles as the ladies of the Friends of Joshua Chamberlain drew in their feet under the chairs they occupied to prevent her from trampling them. She stopped in the center of the room and bowed her head. "Ladies of the jury, I would happily fulfill my civic obligations, despite the hell I suffer in my head, if, if I tell you, it was not for that Jezebel that lurks behind that door!" She pointed to the den, and then reconsidered. "That door!" She pointed to parlor. Not knowing where Adele was maddened her and she crept to the den door and listened through it, then ran to the foyer door and listened through it.

Mrs. Drucker pleaded from her chair she was glued to, "Mrs. Pritchard!"

"NO! No-o-o-o, you do not understand. You do not see. She's not the little waif her whore of a mother left for us to feed. She's not the noble Nancy Nurse she presents for public viewing. I know. I know. When the sun

76

goes down and I'm lying in my sick bed, that little fishwife is making designs on my husband, on yo-o-o-o-ur good doctor!" She pointed a crooked, shaking figure at each lady in the room.

"Mrs. Doctor Albert Pritchard!" It was Miss Jonas who decided enough was enough. She rose from her chair with amazing speed for a woman of her advanced years. She took her walking cane and poked Mrs. Pritchard squarely in the chest with its rubber tip. "That *waif* as you put it is an angel of mercy. Abandoned by her father, orphaned by her mother, she dragged herself up from the gates of hell and made something of herself."

"Gate's of Hell," Mrs. Thomas interjects. "The girl climbed Hardscrabble Hill!" Miss Jonas didn't miss a beat, but made a mental note to remind Mrs. Thomas, at a more opportune time, that, in her day, one did not interrupt their elders.

"Why, when my sister's daughter lay dying of pneumonia, it was Adele who was at her bedside. Not only that, she scrubbed that pigsty they lived in from to top to bottom. She brought groceries to the children, and forced my niece's drunkard husband to pour his whiskey into the outhouse. She even convinced Jack Drucker to take him back at the lumberyard. Jack Drucker!"

Mrs. Drucker started to confirm the last point, but decided against it. Miss Jonas was on a roll.

"That girl," she continued, "is a pillar of this community." Miss Jonas had punctuated each sentence with a poke from the tip of her cane to the now terrified Mrs. Pritchard. "You are a nurse, were a nurse, pretended to be a nurse (three more pokes). And you would *never* soil yourself to drive by that home and throw pills through the window. And as God as my witness, if

77

you ever slander that child in my presence again, I will cane you!" The cane rose in the air. Mrs. Pritchard now backed into a corner, fell into the side table and sent a lamp crashing onto the floor. She leaped to the foyer door and fumbled for the doorknob. She finally secured it, escaped, and ran screaming up the stairs. At the same moment she made her departure, Adele opened the door from the den.

"What in the world is going on in here?" She asked this as sincerely as one who had her ear pressed to the door could manage.

Mrs. Thomas provided the answer. "Miss Jonas was reenacting for Mrs. Pritchard the glorious defeat of the rebel troops at Gettysburg by Maine's own Joshua Chamberlain."

Miss Jonas touched Adele's cheek with the tips of her fingers. "Bless you child." The ladies of the Friends of Joshua Chamberlain exited the Pritchard house never to return to visit Mrs. Pritchard. Adele locked the door when they left, but left the light on for Dr. Pritchard. Then, she climbed the stairs to go to bed. Mrs. Pritchard blocked her way at the top of the stairs. "Where's my husband?" Her voice was low and accusing.

"He told you. He had to go to the island. The Stoner girl is expected to deliver tonight."

"Why didn't you go? Those *are* your people, aren't they?"

"The last one was still born. Dr. Pritchard felt…"

"Oh, it's Dr. Pritchard now! Where were you when that crazed woman attacked me? What have you been doing tonight? I called for you. Why didn't you come to my aid?"

"I didn't know…."

78

Mrs. Pritchard slapped her across the face. "LIAR, she screamed. In her mind Adele could see her hands go around the neck of this horrid shrew. She could see herself squeeze the life out of her. She envisioned herself throwing this bitter hag down the stairs. But, instead, she took the last step up to the landing. Mrs. Pritchard backed up. And Adele calmly said, "Mrs. Pritchard, you're tired."

"Don't patronize me, you whore! One more word and I'll have the sheriff on you. This is my house! Now get my medicine. You've given me a headache." She stormed to her room and slammed the door.

Dr. Pritchard came home as Adele was drawing up morphine in an eyedropper.

"How'd it go," she asked without looking up.

"Another farmer; big one, ten pounds and three ounces..." He walked over and saw the red hand print that was still stinging Adele's face. He cradled her chin in his hand and forced her into the light. "Why did she do this?"

"It's the morphine, Albert. It's making her delusional."

Albert Pritchard knew this wasn't the whole truth. Delusion wasn't the result of morphine; it was the reason for it. His wife had always been a difficult person. She was demanding and critical of him and anyone he associated with. She had plans for them and they did not include a country practice in a small town. She felt she was, and thus he was, meant for bigger things. She grew disappointed, disagreeable, and distraught. And then she became dangerous. He absentmindedly touched his side, where a scar unknown to anyone but the two of them lay. He remembered the night he stitched the one-inch stab wound him self. She had sat crying in a chair

79

watching him. It was the first night he gave her morphine. It was the night he moved her from his bed into the guest room. It was the night he locked the guest room door, as she lay passed out on the bed. It was the night that he told himself if this didn't work...

Dr. Pritchard took the eyedropper and vial out of Adele's hand. He suggested she go to bed and she took his suggestion. He emptied the dropper into the vial, and replaced the vial's stopper. Both were returned to the stainless steel cabinet and locked behind the door. He went to the den and removed an item from the desk drawer and slipped it into his vest pocket. A sad and resigned man climbed the stairs of his home, removed a key from his vest and, for the second time in their marriage, he locked his wife in her room.

The next day Dr. Albert Pritchard put his wife and her suitcase into his Packard and delivered both to the Bangor Home for the Feeble Minded.

Chapter Eight

Albert Pritchard, M.D. had occasion to travel to the insane asylum a few times in the past, but not in this capacity. He brought his wife into the admitting area and they sat in silence. The lack of morphine in her system had already begun to have an effect on her. She was too hoarse to talk, having screamed all the way from Jonasport. Her arms felt like lead pipes from the constant flailing she afflicted on her captor until she could no longer lift them. He was sure he was going to have a black eye and he was still wiping blood from his nose and mouth. He turned a white handkerchief in his hand, looking for a spot to use that wasn't red, as two orderlies came out from behind a locked door. They were large young men with white uniforms. Cloth buttons on the side of their smocks ran up the length of the edge to the shoulder and turned ending at the collar. Neither spoke to him. They came on either side of Mrs. Pritchard and each took her by the elbow and wrist and lifted her from the chair.

"Come with us," one said. She offered no resistance. They escorted her to the door, and the silent one removed a group of keys attached to his belt and unlocked it. "Don't you want to say goodbye to your friend?"

She stared at her husband over her shoulder and croaked, "I hope you and your whore burn in hell."

Dr. Pritchard sat in his chair, shuddering and wiping blood. A nurse wearing a cap for the Piedmont School of Nursing came through the locked door and took the suitcase that lay on the floor next to Dr. Pritchard. She laid it on a table and opened it up.

"We'll have to go through this. Some things are not allowed in the hospital." The some things, he discovered, included brushes, combs, hairpins, mirrors, belts, scarves, button hooks and shoelaces. Basically anything sharp that could be used as a weapon or anything one could fashion into a noose. "Most people aren't aware of the policy." She took a blouse that would have normally been allowed and used it to wrap up the forbidden items. She tied the bundle with the sleeves and handed it to him. "The doctor will be with you shortly," she informed him. Lifting the suitcase, she exited through the locked door, using the keys she pulled from her uniform pocket.

The minute turned into an hour that seemed like a week. By the time the door reopened, Dr. Pritchard had stopped most of the bleeding and was holding the now red colored, handkerchief in the palms of his hands. He didn't know what else to do with it.

"The doctor will see you now." The Piedmont nurse held the door open for him. As he entered the inner sanctum, she said simply, "This way," turned and walked down the hall. She stopped at an office, held another door for him, and when he entered she closed it behind him. The man behind the

82

desk looked like what Dr. Pritchard believed to be the stereotypical psychiatrist. He was a portly man with a body one expects of a person who spends a great deal of time sitting in a chair listening to people talk. He was balding and sported a gray goatee. He smoked a pipe, which he was packing. A crudely made wooden triangle sat on his desk with the name *Charles L Livingston, PhD* roughly cut into the wood. Dr. Pritchard assumed a grateful patient in woodworking class had made it.

"Dr. Pritchard, I presume?"

"I thought it was *Dr. Livingston, I presume.*" He often used humor to mask uneasiness.

"Touché," The psychiatrist returned and pointed to a chair. Dr. Pritchard took his spot in an straight-backed wooden chair in front of the desk. He knew this was purchased for the patients and relatives of patients, comfortable, yet not designed for long-term sitting. Dr. Livingston was seated in a large overstuffed leather swivel chair that rocked back when he leaned into it. It gave him the appearance of a man very at ease in his world. He took a match from a holder, and pointed it at Dr. Pritchard before striking it.

"Do you mind," he asked.

"They're your lungs," the medical doctor advised, implying consent.

"Touché, again." He struck the match and held it to the pipe. He inhaled deeply and let the smoke out slowly. All the while he was looking from Dr. Pritchard's face to the reddened handkerchief the doctor was still clutching in his hands. "So, Dr. Pritchard," he puffed and released the smoke into the air. The small amount of time that lapsed was meant to secure the relative's undivided attention. "Why didn't you have the sheriff bring her in?"

"I couldn't do that to her."

Dr. Livingston took a thin medical folder off the desk in front of him and placed it back on the desk in front of Dr. Pritchard. "Yet, you could do this?" The gesture was an invitation for Dr. Pritchard to open the folder and read it. He eyed it, but did not touch it. He looked into the psychiatrist's face.

"What do you mean?"

Dr. Livingston slid the folder back onto the blotter in front of him, and flipped it opened. He puffed, released, and questioned without looking up. "It says here that you are a general practitioner with an office in your home."

"That's correct."

"And you have been treating your wife for sometime for migraine headaches. And that your prescribed treatment is morphine."

"That is correct."

"Did you bring her patient records?"

"No, I didn't". Dr. Pritchard corrected himself. "I don't have records of it. She's my wife. Whom would I possibly make a record for?"

"Me?" Dr. Livingston posed as he puffed. Dr. Pritchard sat silent. Dr. Livingston suggested, "Shouldn't you say *touché*?"

An angry husband rose indignantly from his chair, toppling it onto the floor. "Damn you, man. This isn't a game!"

"Dr. Pritchard," the psychiatrist said calmly, "please sit down. And lower your voice. This *is* a hospital." Dr. Pritchard regained his self-control, righted the chair, and sat in it. *This was a mistake,* he thought. *He thinks this is all about the morphine. He doesn't see that she had a mental problem.*

Surely, he talked to her. Surely, he had to see it. He suddenly wished he had examined that folder. He looked at Dr. Livingston.

"I don't like your accusatory tone."

"I don't make accusations, sir. I make observations. As a physician, you must know that medicine is not an exact science. Psychiatric medicine is even less exact." He waved his hand around the office. "There are no bandages here I can apply, no salves I can rub in to the psyche. No scalpel can probe into the subconscious. I can't very well go and ask your wife where it hurts. This is what I know. One, she is very angry. Two, you have addicted her to morphine. Three, the damage is done. If you would have brought her here sooner, maybe, but now all I can do is try to pick up the pieces. How extensive is the damage? I do not know. What I can salvage, and what has already been destroyed is anybody's guess. Narcotic drugs affect both the mind and body. To help, if I can help her, I need answers. You will provide them." He tossed a tablet on the desk in front of Dr. Pritchard. He drew on his pipe to no avail and tapped it annoyingly into an ashtray. "I need to know when it started. What were the symptoms of these alleged headaches in the beginning, during the course of your treatment and now? What were the dosage, method, and frequency of the morphine use in the beginning, during the course of your treatment and now?"

"Dr. Livingston, morphine is not her only problem, surely you must see that. And if you can't, I believe my best course of action is to take her out of here, and find someone who can."

"Dr. Pritchard, *Me thinks thou dost protest too much.* I believe I am a better judge of mental illness than you. I believe your wife's problem stems from the drug addiction you led her into. And I believe it is in her best interest that I commit her to this institution. You have no say in the matter. She is from now until the time I discharge her in the protection of the State of Maine. You have no say in the matter! In two months time, I will get her to a point where she can be released. Then you can start to make what repairs are possible to her body… if you still have a license to practice medicine." He tapped his pipe on the tablet spilling tobacco residue on it. "Now write. When you are through, leave it on my desk. I have patients to see." That said, he rose from his desk with an air of authority, and left the room.

Dr. Pritchard sat for a few moments taking in all the man had said. Then, with a shaking hand, he removed a pen from the inkwell and started to write.

On his way home, he was tortured with the information that he wrote on the tablet. Anger, sadness, doubt, concern, and guilt raced around in his head. Was he right and the psychiatrist mistaken, or inept? Was he the inept one? Guilt won out over the other emotions. He, a physician, had addicted a healthy patient to a narcotic drug for the purpose of shutting her up and living in peace in his home. Not just a patient, but also his wife. He murmured in a low voice, "My God, My God, what had he done?" The last thing he noticed as he left Livingston's office was a plaque on the wall with the Hippocratic Oath, the same oath he had hanging in his parlor. A passage from it jumped off the wall and burned into his psyche. He was so intently into his anguish that he failed to notice the ice truck backing out of Wilbur's market into the street. He struck it at full speed. When the sheriff and ambulance driver pulled him from the wreckage, he was mumbling over and over, "I will do no harm."

Chapter Nine

Little Edwin Tyler was bored with swinging on the rope tied to a tree at Dots Pond. He watched the other boys take their turns and noticed that when they released the rope they were only about three feet off the water. He looked back across the dirt road that bordered the lake. He struck upon a novel idea. *Yeah,* he thought, *this is gonna be great.* He ran to a tree across the road and climbed the first two branches.

"Hand me the rope," he called to his swimming companions. When the end of the rope was handed up to him, he climbed as high into the tree as the length of the rope would allow. He stood on a branch and to the shouts of encouragement from his peers he jumped. *This is gonna be great!* It was not so great. His trajectory was off just slightly and instead of hitting the lake, he hit the tree. He laid motionless half on the bank and half in the water.

"Is he dead?"

"I don't think so, his chest is moving."

"Should we tell somebody?"

"If we do, we're gonna get a licking."

"If we don't and he dies, we're gonna get a worse licking."

"Yeah."

That decided they did paper, rock, and scissors to decide who would go and who would stay. The loser stayed. It was better to tell and run home, than to stay and be here when help arrived. The stayer would get the most questions. The winner ran back to town and told Big Ed.

Nurse Abbott heard the telephone ring, stop, ring again moments later, but ignored it. Edwin Tyler had brought his son in and she was busying picking pieces of bark out of the side of his face with tweezers. He stood relatively still for that, but when Nurse Abbott went to apply the iodine, he thrashed so that he knocked the bottle over spilling it in her lap. His father relayed to her that the young scalawag who fetched him said he was *knocked out cold*, but the child was awake and crying when he showed up. She had checked his pupils for proper dilation in the light and rotated his various limbs to see if anything was broken. Giving him a clean bill of health, she cleaned him up and scolded him about the dangers of foolhardiness. Big Ed paid her in cash and frowned at his expensive son. She sent Little Ed on his way to be whipped by his father or coddled by his mother, depending on who ruled the roost. She had just escorted the two Eds off the porch when Sheriff Farnham pulled up. She started telling him the now funny tale of youthful daredevilry before he made it up the stairs.

He tried to interrupt her. "I've been trying to call you, Nurse Abbott."

"Yes, I was busy picking bark out of a young man's face. He was trying to turn himself into a human maypole, but he struck the pole. If he hadn't, he would have been a half a mile in the air before..." Sheriff Farnham grabbed her by the wrist in an attempt to halt her tongue.

"There's been an accident!"

Albert had already been admitted to the floor when she arrived. She stopped a nurse in the hall.

"Excuse me," she inquired. "Do you know what room Dr. Pritchard is in?"

The woman looked her up and down. "Ask at the nurse's station", she coldly replied. And then, she walked away. Adele looked at the stain on her uniform and wished she had taken time to change. She followed the direction she was given.

"Excuse me...excuse me." None of the nurses looked up

A plump lady in a pink dress stepped up to the counter. "May I help you?"

"Yes, I'm looking for Albert Pritchard."

"Are you a relative," an older nurse asked.

"No, I'm his nurse." The other nurses giggled and whispered to each other. Sunday school class, again. The older nurse turned to the pink lady.

"Show the doctor's *assistant* to his room." The pink lady came into the hall and waved for Nurse Abbott to follow her.

"Don't pay any attention to those snobs," she advised. "They think anyone who didn't go to nursing school isn't a real nurse." Adele was stunned. She had been at Dr. Pritchard's side for over five years. How long had these girls gone to their school? Not only had that she delivered babies. Had any of them ever done that? She was angry, but when she walked into Albert's room, her anger melted. His right leg was in a cast and his face was bandaged so that if she didn't see his name on his bed, she would not have known him. His torso was wrapped up. He was either asleep or sedated. She pulled a chair up next to the bed, sat, and took his hand. She stayed in that position until one of the hospital nurses came down and coldly told her that visiting hours were over.

With Dr. Pritchard lying with a broken leg and broken spirit in the Soctomah County Hospital, the office was closed. A sign on the door and on the bulletin boards at the various town halls in the county directed his patients to the nearest alternate physician. Some would have to travel a great distance. Adele had no intention of closing the office. She had covered the practice on his yearly fishing trips to northern Maine and on the times he took his cold fish of a wife on retreats to Cape Cod. However, as Adele learned on her next visit, his fellow physicians warned him of the dangers and legalities of a nurse practicing medicine without a license. So despite her objections, he insisted and she complied with his wishes. On the third visit she wore a plain cotton dress, if for no other reason, to avoid the glares of the capped nurses. Although she did not realize it, she would not be wearing her uniform for a long time.

Albert's doctor explained the extent of his injuries, and the depression he had slipped into as a result of the accident. He warned her to be prepared for an extensive hospital stay.

After her training period, Albert had given her a salary. And with her room and board provided, she banked her money. Nonetheless, with the closing of the practice, Adele decided that it would be wise to cut expenses. One of the expenses she felt she could do without was having someone prepare her meals, so she let the cook go. Millie Blake had been with the Pritchard's for years, but was quite fond of Adele and sympathetic to her plight. She took it well.

One life-altering night, after returning home from visiting Albert, Adele was in the kitchen making corn chowder. It was her mother's recipe, and she had not made it since the sardine factory. She had cut up the potatoes and onions, and had cut the corn off the cob. She was getting ready to heat the cream when she heard a loud thump on the porch. She looked out the kitchen window but saw nothing. Then she heard quick footsteps retreating into the distance. She ran to the parlor and looked out the front window. She spied two men wearing the type of clothing common to merchant sailors. They had just left the yard and were rounding horny corner (this was the name given to the bend in the road by the entrance to the former Jonas Sardine Factory). She ran out to call after them and tripped on something lying on the porch. It proved to be a young man about her age. He had cropped blond hair and the bluest eyes she had ever seen. He wasn't fully conscious, but enough to press his bloodied hands into his abdomen, and he winced in pain as he did. She propped open the screen door with a rocker and dragged his rigid body into the parlor. As he lay there on the floor, she grabbed a towel off the stack in the kitchen. She knelt by him and unbuttoned his shirt. She saw through the blood a round hole in his side the size of a nickel. She crammed the towel in it and pressed down on it. By now the young man had lost consciousness completely. Adele gathered a pan of water, soap and an abdominal dressing. She cleaned and dressed his wound, but with much more care and skill than she did for the man with the wounded arm so many years ago, on her first night in the house. And this was an entirely different situation; this man could die. Under different circumstances, Adele would have treated the man. But, she knew that now the difference between capable and legal. She stood to go call the sheriff. The young man stirred and she looked down at him.

"Hello," he said weakly.

"You've been hurt. I'm going to call the sheriff. He'll send an ambulance and you can go to the hospital."

"No, please, they'll put me in jail." He passed out again.

"I'm sorry," she said to the unconscious boy. "I have to." She wasn't going to jeopardize her freedom to help him secure his. Besides if he feared the law, he must have done something. She went into the den to place her call. Then she stopped, went back and looked down on him. She dropped slowly to her knees, resting her backsides on the heels of her feet. She laid her hands in her lap and studied his face. This boy was not a criminal. She didn't know how she knew. But she knew. She reached out and touched his face, just to be sure. She stood, bent over, and took him by a wrist and an ankle. Using a maneuver she had read about in the U S Army's Medical Corpsman Training Manual, she squatted by him, lifted him up and over her shoulder, stood and carried him up the stairs. She could barely walk with him, and had to stop on each step to regain the strength to rise to the next step. Her back ached and she was out of breath by the time she crested the top of the stairway. But she succeeded. She deposited him in the patient room. And despite Dr. Pritchard's advice and the warnings of his fellow physicians, despite the laws of the State of Maine regarding a nurse without a cap who practices medicine without a license, she was back in business.

Adele checked to see if the movement resulted in the re-occurrence of bleeding. When she was sure that it had not, she hurried down the stairs. She returned with a stainless steel instrument tray which she had placed all the material she knew to be necessary to perform her forbidden task, and then she returned the room with the little cherubs on the wall. She filled the stainless washbasin she had laid on top of the pile with warm water from the bathroom sink. Carefully she removed his shirt and the bandage she had applied while he laid on the parlor floor. When she had scrubbed the open wound and area around it, she shaved the cleaned spot to prevent hair from being trapped inside and causing an infection. She carefully removed the cap of a bottle of ether and poured a small amount of it onto a gauze pad. The pad was placed over his mouth and nose for a brief period. She waited for it to take affect, and then pinched him in the neck. When he flinched, she repeated the process. When the pinching no longer elicited a response, she went into the bathroom and washed her hands. The only thing that remained on the instrument tray was a sterilized package wrapped in a towel, the corners tucked in to prevent it from falling open. She tugged on the fold and laid the corner back. Taking the remaining corners with her index finger and thumb, she laid each corner open. She slid one hand partially into a rubber glove that had been placed on top of the instruments. She picked up the other glove with

93

her partially gloved hand and donned it. Then she used her gloved hand to completely glove the first. She followed this peculiar method to ensure that her task would be performed in a sterile field.

Using a pair of hemostats and her fingers, she probed and inspected the wound. The blade of a knife did not cause it. Nor was it caused by anything very sharp as the edges of the cut were torn and jagged. Adele deduced that a stick or a pipe caused the wound. Maybe he had fallen on something trying to escape the law. He was a lucky young man. The penetration wasn't deep and no organs were damaged.

Nurse Abbott took a pair of scissors and trimmed the jagged edges. Then she laced a piece of four ought catgut onto a half round needle. Using the hemostats to grasp the needle she inserted it into the outer edge of the wound and through the torn flap of skin. She made two loops of the catgut over the tip of the hemostats. She unclasped the instrument, clamped it again on the tip of the needle and pulled the knot down to the skin. A pair of scissors was used to cut the suture and the first stitch was complete. She repeated this process eight times across the opening, dabbing the blood leaking from the hole as she did. She worked as quickly as she could, knowing he could wake from the ether-induced sleep anytime.

When she was through she cleaned up the room and patient and got him ready for bed. She stood in the doorway looking at his face before turning off the light. Then she went to bed herself, and saw that face in her dreams. She never made her corn chowder.

The following morning, she was making breakfast in the kitchen when she heard him calling.

"Hello. Hello, anybody here? Hel-lo-o!" She climbed the stairs carrying a breakfast tray. Entering the patient room, she walked over and placed it on his lap.

"Good morning, sir. How are we feeling this morning?"

"...Fine as frog hair. Am I in the hospital?" He tore into the eggs and bacon, as young men are known to do.

"No, you're in the home of Dr. Albert Pritchard. Your friends dumped you on the porch last night. Apparently, they had neither the time nor inclination to take you to the hospital." Adele leaned against the wall and crossed her arms. "Do you want to tell me what happened?"

He glanced up at her between bites and shrugged his shoulders.

"Same old story; merchant ship comes to port. The local yokels are afraid we're gonna take their girls. Some of them jump us. One of them cracked me on the side of the head with a piece of lead pipe.... Then, he rammed the broken end into my gut."

"Lead pipe," she repeated, nodding her head. She was glad she gave him a tetanus shot.

"What?"

"Nothing," she replied. She probed his mind now as she probed his wound last night. "Do you want me to call the sheriff?"

"Oh, no ma'am, I don't want to involve the law".

"Why not, you didn't do anything. You're the victim here?"

"Miss..."

"Adele."

"Adele, that's a pretty name. But you should have a pretty name, you're a pretty lady." Adele felt her face redden. "You see, Adele, I'm a sailor. I'm from away. It's always our fault. I've got two months before I ship out. I don't want to spend that two months sitting in a cell waiting for justice to be served." Adele smiled a little smile, happy to learn that he was no fugitive. He took a large gulp of orange juice. He started to wipe the residue off of his lip with his forearm. But he stopped himself and picked up the napkin she had placed on the tray. He clumsily wiped the pulp from his mouth. "I'd rather spend it with a pretty lady with a pretty name."

Adele smiled a big smile. "You, sir, are a flirt."

He ignored this. "Well, you're not the doctor. So who are you?"

"I'm his..." She paused, torn between her attraction for this young man and the need protect herself. "I'm his daughter. He had to go out. He told me to tell you that you could leave whenever you feel up to it."

He peeked under the sheets. "Uh, I can't go out like this. I *will* get arrested." The red color in her face deepened. Her face felt warm. She felt peculiar and could not understand why. Was it him? She chased the thought from her mind.

"Yes," she said, turned and opened the door to a cedar wardrobe. "That wouldn't do at all." She took his clothes out and laid them on the bed. "We washed them for you. They were covered in blood. And I stitched up the hole in your shirt."

"Thank you, Adele."

"You're welcome..."

"Harry. Harry Wallace. He tipped an imaginary hat.

"You're welcome, Harry Wallace. I'll leave you to dress." She began to feel her face cool again, and was relieved.

She left the room and, halfway down the steps, she stopped and mouthed the name, "Harry Wallace." The heat in her face returned.

Harry Wallace left and returned later in the day to pay for the services that were rendered. He returned the next day and the day that followed to try and thank the doctor in person. Each day Adele made an excuse for the doctor's absence. Each day Adele and Harry sat on the porch and talked for a while. On the fourth visit Adele made the excuse that Dr. Pritchard had gone to Boston for a medical convention. They sat on the porch that night and talked until ten o'clock. The following day he stopped by to ask Adele to go roller-skating. To her surprise she heard herself say yes, and, at twenty years of age, Adele Susannah Abbott went on her first date.

When they walked into the roller rink all talk ceased. Slowly people started to whisper to each other and smile. Some came up and greeted Adele and asked to be introduced to her handsome escort. Everyone was surprised and delighted to see her out. She deserved it. Harry showed her how to skate and she picked it up as quickly as when Albert showed her how to drive. Soon she was skating around to the music. She stumbled a little, but never fell, even when Harry put her at the end of the whip. When the evening came to a close, everyone came up and told them goodbye. And please come back again.

On their third date Harry took Adele to the Saturday dance at the community hall. Saturday morning found Adele at the Style Emporium. Alice gave her a special hairdo for the occasion. As she admired her self in the mirror, a sudden fear came over her. She lowered her head and stated, "I'm going tell him that I can't go."

"…You're what?" Alice saw the worry in Adele's face. She took her by the hands and set her down in the beauty throne. "Tell Alice what's going on in that head of yours." Adele held back her tears.

"I don't know how to dance. Harry had to teach me to skate. I don't what him to know that I can't dance either. I'll look like…well, like an old maid."

Alice closed the shop earlier than usual. She turned on the radio and showed Adele the latest dance steps. They were all "the latest" for Adele, who had never danced a step in her life.

Harry showed up early and waited in the sitting room for her to get ready. He stood up when she glided down the stairs and entered the room..

"My God, Adele, you're beautiful."

"And you, Harry Wallace, are still a flirt. Shall we go?"

They arrived at the hall and entered like visiting royalty. All eyes were on them as Harry escorted her to the floor and led her in a dance. It was an evening she would never forget. When he dropped her off at her house and escorted her to the porch, they sat and Adele told him the truth about the day they met.

"Nurses without caps practicing medicine without a license can go to prison in the state of Maine."

Harry grabbed his side and groaned.

"Oh, am I going to die?"

"You are not funny. This is serious." Harry looked into her eyes. He dared to kiss her. She dared to let him. Something stirred deep inside her. At that moment her feelings for men changed. Papa, the whispering boys in her Sunday school class, and Tibias Anderson evaporated from her psyche. They were replaced by the knight in shining armor that she had introduced to the town as Harry Wallace, merchant sailor.

"See you tomorrow?" Harry asked.

"See you tomorrow," Adele confirmed. She went into the house and watched through the window as he walked off. Then she twirled and danced from the parlor to sitting room, on to the den and into the kitchen, back to the parlor and off again.

Chapter Ten

With the practice closed Adele had plenty of time to visit Albert. Yet with a new man in her life, her visits decreased. She hadn't told him about Harry. Albert had but three rules for her living in the house, and she didn't want him to know that she had broken even one. Besides he was so despondent she feared how any type of news might affect him. She decided to tell him at a more appropriate time. She excused her reduction in visits as an uncomfortable feeling she got from the nurses at the hospital.

"They hate me."

"They hate themselves, Adele." He tried to comfort her. "They know you've learned more without school than any of them learned with it. I miss seeing you in your uniform. It seems strange."

"I miss wearing it." They had been in the solarium. She was pushing him in a wicker wheelchair down the hall and into his room. The floor nurse, fresh from school and, as Dr. Pritchard put it, *as green as a cucumber,* came rushing into the room.

"Wait a minute," green nurse announced, "I'll help him into the bed. With his injuries, this is no job for visitors." Angry, Dr. Pritchard pushed her aside, got out of the wheelchair, and set himself on the bed. He slung his good leg, then his casted leg onto the bed. The newly capped nurse went to the foot of the bed and felt the toes protruding beyond the plaster.

"Doctor, your toes are hot and very red. Now this could be a sign of infection, or perhaps poor circulation."

"Not quite, dear," the former Nurse Abbott corrected. "Hot toes with a foul odor would be a sign of infection. Cold, blue toes *could* indicate poor circulation. Warm, red toes; blanket on foot in solarium." Nurse Cucumber left the room embarrassed. Albert laugh and Adele was pleased to see him do it.

"Well," said Albert when he stopped laughing, "I'll be home soon, you'll be in your uniform, and things will be back to normal." Then, he thought about his wife. The joy of Adele's visit passed from him and depression again attacked him. On the way home Adele wondered if things would ever be back to normal.

Harry was sitting on the porch when she pulled into the drive.

"How's your father?" He chuckled.

"Please Harry, that's cruel," she cried.

He took her hands and set her in one of the rockers. He squatted on his hunches and apologized. "I'm sorry. How is he?"

"The doctor said his ribs are healed. There will be some scarring on his face. He had a lot of stitches."

"They should have let you put them in," he said, lifting his shirt to show off her handiwork. She tucked his shirt back into the front of his pants. He gasped quietly as she did.

"His leg will be a long time healing. The problem is the depression he's in. They believe it's a result of the accident. I think it's his wife. I don't know if he'll ever recover."

"Of course he will. And you'll help him. Everyone says you're the Florence Nightintime of Jonasport, whoever she is."

"Nightingale," Adele corrected. "She was a famous nurse from the Civil War. She founded the American Red Cross. And how do you suddenly know what everyone in town says. You're from away."

"I've met some folks. I get around. Why just yesterday I met Jack Drucker. He offered me a job in the lumberyard."

Adele threw his hands down. "Harry, you don't mean it. Don't tease me. What about all that gruff about "man o' the sea" and "call no port me home.""

"That was before you. Adele, my commitment is up after this voyage. You know I ship out tomorrow."

"I don't want to talk about it." She tried to pout, but not being used to the expression, it came out looking like a severely swollen lower lip. He took one finger and pushed the fleshy fold back to its normal state.

"Now Adele, we talked about this."

"But you said Jack offered you a job. Can't you just quit now?"

"I made a commitment and a Wallace is good for his word. You would not want to marry a liar, would you?"

It was a good statement. It showed the quality of the man making it. However, Adele didn't hear it. She heard only one word and she repeated it.

"Marry?"

Harry came up on one knee and assumed the traditional position. He pulled a small velvet-covered box from his pocket. He laid it in his palm and opened it with his other hand, offering it up for her inspection.

"Miss Adele Susannah Abbott, it would give me great honor and everlasting joy if you would consent to join me in the holy bond of matrimony." And thus he gave the speech he had rehearsed twenty-seven times in front of the mirror at the boarding house and twice walking up her drive.

Adele gazed down at the box and viewed a small gold band and a ring next to it with the world's smallest diamond. Her throat began to burn. Her face flushed hot. Her chest began to heave and her lungs released an audible shudder. She threw her arms around her fiancée and burst into tears. It wasn't the reaction he expected. Adele was a calm and rational, no nonsense woman. She would either say no kindly or say yes. In his rehearsal proposal, she would say, "yes Mr. Harry Wallace, I accept your proposal of marriage". He would then slip the ring on her finger (left hand, third finger, left hand, third finger), kiss her, and make his exit. He prayed he would not trip and fall down the steps.

After a few minutes of her squeezing the air out of his lungs, he asked, "Is this a yes?" She released him and took the engagement ring from its bed and slipped it onto the third finger of her left hand.

Harry sprang to his feet. "Yah-hoo! Yah-h-ho-o-o!" He did a gig on the porch in front of God and all His witnesses. While Harry was dancing, Adele was thinking. The thought came to her. She had to ensure that he would come home from the sea. She had to secure his love and their future. She would trade his ring for her virginity. She rose and took him by the hand. He silently followed her into the house, and up to her room. That night, in her grandmother's bed, in direct violation of rule number three, she gave the little boy in the picture on her wall another secret to whisper about.

Adele woke up the following morning at four. At first she was startled at the man lying next to her. But then she settled into his warmth and kissed him on the cheek. He stirred but did not wake. She tossed back her covers and saw a small amount of blood on the bed. She threw them back over her and got out of bed by slipping out from under them. Washing herself in the bathroom, she cursed her stupidity. She was a nurse. She knew that when the hymen broke, hemorrhaging occurred. Why hadn't she made some kind of preparations? But, then she corrected her thinking? What could she have done? *Excuse me fiancée; do you mind waiting to deflowering me until I put a rubber sheet on the bed? I so hate to soil my grandmother's mattress.* She was brushing her hair out and another thought struck her. *Oh my God... his penis! It'll be covered in blood. Does he know? Of course, he knows, he's a man. Men knew these things. Don't they?*

"He probably knows," she told the woman in the mirror. She decided against going into the bedroom and rapped on the door. "Harry, get up," she said and hurried down the stairs. She was making breakfast when she heard him walking on the floor above her. Then as she put on the coffee, she heard him running water into the tub.

The coffee was ready when he came downstairs. She had no idea how he took it, so she left it black. When he came into the kitchen, dressed and ready to leave, he had a look of apprehension on his face. But it disappeared when she smiled and handed him the coffee. As he was sipping it, she offered to take him to the docks.

"That'll be great. It's a long walk." He started drinking his coffee a little faster. "Well, the sun will be up soon. I'd better get going. No sense giving folks something to talk about."

"It's a small town," she admitted.

"Yep," he said and handed her the empty cup. He kissed her and left the house without the security of the porch light. When he was gone she looked into the empty cup.

"Yep," she said, mimicking him. "Black it is."

She was punctual picking him up. Goodbyes being difficult for both of them, they rode to the docks in silence. Right before they turned into the drive, Harry broke the silence.

"So, being a nurse and all, I guess you knew about the blood?" She turned to look at him and he was studying his shoes.

"And, being a man o' the sea, I assume you knew."

"I heard some talk. I'm sorry about the sheets." He was still looking down.

Those must be some interesting shoes. "Its okay, Harry, it'll come out."

"Yeah, but I'm sorry anyway."

"Harry, you don't have to…."

"I love you, Adele."

"I love you, Harry."

Adele didn't know why she thought she would be the only woman at the ship. She guessed she assumed that all merchant sailors were from away. But she learned that many shipping out on the *Sovereign State* called Soctomah County their home. Harry kissed her. Adele clung to his embrace, and briefly squeezed him tighter when she felt him pull away. Then, she released him. He boarded the ship as Adele joined the other fiancées, girlfriends, and wives at the edge of the dock. Most of the older women left as soon as they saw their men off. Adele assumed it was old hat for them, and shuddered at the thought. But many others stayed and watched that whore of a ship take the love of their lives out to sea. When it was no more than a speck on the horizon, they dispersed. They threw glances at one another and gave understanding nods. Then, they went to their separate homes to pray for a safe passage.

Chapter Eleven

Winter had come to Maine and the first snow of the season had fallen on Jonasport. It wasn't a bad storm, just enough to blanket the ground and leave the trees white. Adele was taking the rockers off the porch and storing them for the season in the cellar. She had brought the first through the bulkhead when she noticed the near empty coal bin.

"Oh my God", she cried. In all the commotion in her recent life, she had failed to order any coal. She ran upstairs and phoned Mr. Thomas.

"No dear," he laughed. "It won't be any problem at all…No dear, it's my fault. Albert always orders before now. I should have had the forethought to call…No problem at all. I'll get it and be right over."

Mr. Thomas arrived, drove his truck around back, and shoveled the coal into the outside bin. He offered to shovel it through the chute into the cellar, but Adele declined his offer. The hired man would do it, thank you just the same. Mr. Thomas knew she had let go of the hired man the same as the cook. But he didn't let on. As he was leaving and pulled out the drive, he caught a glimpse of her in the mirror. She was heading to the shed to get the coal shovel. He simultaneously cursed and blessed her Yankee pride.

She had just finished this chore and was in the bathroom washing the coal dust off when the telephone rang. *Harry* she thought. But Harry wasn't due back for at least three weeks.

"Please hold the line for Soctomah County Hospital," the operator asked. "Go ahead with your call," she told the party on the other end.

"Hello. Am I addressing Albert Pritchard's *assistant.*" It was the haughty head nurse who made Adele so uncomfortable.

An annoyed Adele responded. "I don't mind you referring to me as an assistant, but could you possible display a little decorum and professional courtesy by referring to him as Dr. Pritchard?"

"*Doctor* Pritchard is being discharged. Could you *assist* him by coming and picking him up?" She heard a click in the telephone, and then the line went dead...

Adele got ready as quickly as she could. She donned her black wool overcoat with rabbit collar, and put on her overshoes and rabbit earmuffs. As she donned her doeskin gloves her engagement ring caught her eye. She ran upstairs and opened a dresser drawer. A sudden sense of betrayal invaded her as she took out the box with the other ring, removed the one off her hand (just for now) and replaced in the box. She slipped the box back in the midst of her unmentionables, donned her gloves and headed out of the house.

It had started to snow. She knew the weather would delay her travel and had a picture in her head of the capped nurses shoving Albert out the front door the minute the doctor signed his discharge. She was going too fast for the road conditions and slid sideways as she turned off the town road onto the Boston Post Road. She slowed her car and drove carefully the remainder of the trip. When she arrived and didn't see Albert shivering in the parking lot, she parked the Ford and went into the hospital. She went through the front door and headed towards the hospital's patient rooms. A nurse intercepted her in the hall, extending her arm in the stop gesture as if she were directing traffic.

"Dr. Pritchard has been discharged. We called you an hour ago. He's in the doctors' lounge talking to his wife's psychiatrist. You'll have to wait in the lobby." Adele said nothing, turned on her heels and headed for the lobby. The nurse let out a huff and she, too, turned on her heels.

Adele sat fuming in one of the chairs in the lobby. She caught an unsettling glimpse from the corner of her eye of the latest copy of the *Soctomah County Crier* lying on the chair next to her. She looked away, her brain refusing to register what he eyes saw. She stood up and stepped away from it hoping the bold headline would change before she looked again. She turned around, stepped forward, bent over, and picked up the paper. The headline read *Tragedy At Sea.* She closed her eyes, opened them slowly and read it again. It did not change. Not yet convinced she scanned the article. *Twin-Screw Steamship Sovereign State*...She gasped and released the air... *winter storm was not expected*...Please Lord, please. *Rescue attempt*...God no. *No survivors.* Black surrounded her field of vision diminishing to a point to where she could only see the last two words. Then they too, disappeared. She felt herself weaving, her stomach churning. Then she felt nothing.

When Adele awoke she was sitting on the floor, a man was holding her up. She heard the echo of a woman asking her if she had been drinking. Then she heard the same voice without the echo.

"Has your Dr. Pritchard been providing you with morphine, too?"

Suddenly Adele woke from her semi-conscious state. She sprang to her feet. The accusing nurse took three steps back, which were matched by Adele's three steps forward.

"Shut-your-asinine-mouth, you god damned pompous witch!" Witch was followed by a stream of projectile vomit that covered the uniform, face, and Fairfield College Nursing cap of the offending nurse. Adele ran into the bathroom and vomited again.

Dr. Pritchard had finished his call and wheeled himself into the lobby just as Adele was coming out of the bathroom. The lobby was empty except for a janitor who was mopping vomit up off the floor. Albert hugged her, and she him. As they left the lobby Albert pointed to the mess on the floor.

"Do you suppose that came from a child with a virus in his stomach, or a woman with a child in her stomach?" His laugh was forced.

When Adele left the hospital that day, she never returned to Soctomah County hospital, or any other. Upon the event of her death, it may be said that whatever illness or injury may overtake her; the cause of her death can be directly related to a *staff* infection.

The snow was accumulating in the parking lot and Adele had to struggle to push Albert across it to the car. She would have just left the wheelchair where it sat after she loaded Albert. But she needed a moment. She returned it to the lobby and left it in the same spot she had left her last meal. She picked up the paper and felt the tears welling in her eyes. She choked them back, folded the paper, and slipped it under her coat. "There will be time for this," she said, not realizing she was speaking. "My Harry is gone. Albert is alive. And he needs me."

Chapter Twelve

Adele didn't know what to talk about on the way home. She wanted to tell Albert about Harry, even more now than before. But she didn't.

"What did Dr. Livingston say about Mrs. Pritchard?"

Albert was optimistic. "She's getting better every day. He thinks she should be able to come home by spring." In the summer the man had said two months.

Adele was torn between her devotion to Albert and her dislike for his wife. Devotion won out. "Oh that's good. I'm so glad."

"Watch the road, Adele."

Her next topic of conversation surprised even her. "Albert, do you know what a sampler is?"

"What?" He looked at her puzzled.

"A sampler, I made one as a child. You sew letters on a piece of cloth. Momma had me make one to learn my alphabet."

"That's nice, Adele. Watch the road." He was understandably concerned about riding in a car. "These winter roads are greasy. You'll lose control before you know it. Slow down some, please." She slowed.

"Well", she continued. "I've taken it up as a hobby. You know, just something to wile away the hours…"

"The road, Adele, watch the road."

By the time they came into Jonasport the snow was so thick that Adele had a difficulty seeing the road. Albert wasn't seeing at all. He had long since closed his eyes and had a death grip on the dashboard with one hand, and the armrest with the other. They pulled into the drive and Adele veered off and pulled the car right up to the front door.

"Don't Adele, you'll get stuck."

"I won't. There are fewer steps to get up at the front."

She made it to the door with minimal spinning of the tires, jumped out and helped him hobble to the door, being careful not to let him get his foot wet. Albert wanted to try to make it up the stairs to his room, but she wouldn't have it and detoured into the sitting room. She helped him off with his coat, took his hat off of his head and tossed them both onto the Queen Anne chair.

"Sit," she ordered. He sat and she lifted and rolled his legs around onto the sofa, forcing him to recline. Pillows placed behind his neck and an afghan around his feet were the finishing touches. "There," she said pleased.

She went out through the front door and got into the car. Trying to reverse the path she took up didn't work. She got stuck. After throwing the transmission from forward to reverse and back again, pushing the gas pedal to the floor after every shift, she finally made it to the drive and parked the Ford in his normal spot. She knew she must have torn up a lot of turf in the process and dreaded seeing it in the spring.

She came in though the back door with an armload of firewood. When she dropped it on the hearth she heard him mumble, "I told you." She ignored the comment. She opened the damper. After laying some kindling on the grate and placing crumpled paper under it, she held a struck match to it. When the flame reached the kindling, she blew on it until the tenders ignited. When the fire reached a point to her satisfaction, she placed some logs on the grate in just the right spot to ensure a good airflow. She stood up and admired her fire-making skills.

"It's warm enough in here with the furnace. You don't need to bother with that." Adele didn't know if it was concern or just something to say. She didn't turn to face him, but spoke into the fire.

"Nothing makes a body feel at home like a good fire in the hearth." She placed another log on the fire and, satisfied, took his hat and coat and left. She returned carrying a pair of crutches. She had previously adjusted them to the size she thought he would need. She leaned them against the wall next to the sofa.

"These are for you *if* you *have* to get up." She pointed a finger at him in all her nursing glory.

"Yes, Nurse Abbott."

She brushed the dampness of his overcoat off the Queen Anne chair, straightened her dress and sat. She folded her hands in her lap and prepared to tell him about Harry. She didn't get a chance.

"When's Millie getting here? I'm so sick of hospital food I could die. Those people boil everything." She knew the feeling. Since the practice closed she had been living out of a boiling pot, the only way she knew how to cook.

"I had to let her go."

"You did what? Why, for the love of God? She's been with me for years."

"Albert," she explained. "After we closed the doors, I had no income. I had to let her go. And the hired man, too."

"You let Malcolm go, too?" He paused and broke out laughing.

"I don't see what's so funny."

"My dear, Adele," he said shaking his head. "And to think, Isabelle thought you were after my money. And you didn't even know I had any."

"Isabelle?"

"Mrs. Pritchard. Yes, I guess you were never told her name. I think she's probably forgotten it. Hated it with a passion, she did, Isabelle Gong. When she was a child, the other children would tease her something awful. *It's a bell, gong!* Get it?" He swung his arms like an oriental swinging the big hammer in the pictures of Tibet. Adele got it. "Yes sir. But she liked the name Pritchard. Wore it like a badge, *Mrs. Pritchard,* or sometimes, *Mrs. Dr. Albert Pritchard.*" Adele remembered Miss Jonas calling her that while poking her with a cane. Albert rose up on the sofa. "But that's another story for another day." Guilt had overtaken him again. He turned his head, closed his eyes, and temporarily sent the guilt away. "What I was about to say is that I've invested well. And not in that fool stock market." He shoved the crutches under his arms and headed into the den. "I've got an egg farm in

Joshua, dairy cows in Perry, and potatoes up in Scotia County. I'll never be wealthy, but I guess we can afford a pork roast." He leaned against his desk and picked up the telephone. "Vonnie, Albert Pritchard...fine, and you? And it's good to be home. Thank you. Ring the Blakes' for me, will you?"

They didn't have pork roast that night. Millie showed up with a nice fish. They had baked salmon and all the trimmings. It tasted so good to them, both being denied epicurean pleasure for so long. They devoured their meal in silence. When the silence became noticeable, they peered at each other over their plates and laughed. And they were happy.

Chapter Thirteen

Adele vomited again the next morning, and again the following morning. She checked in on Albert, because she would have to help him downstairs. He was still sleeping, so she went downstairs and stuffed soda crackers in her mouth to ease the nausea. She didn't need to kill a rabbit to know what was wrong. She was with child.

Her queasiness had passed by the time Albert woke up and prepared to meet the day. He had his breakfast (welcome back Millie), and told Adele she should eat something. She declined. With the morning meal out of the way, he had Adele drive him about to the town halls of the county to post a flier.

Albert Pritchard, M.D. having returned from the hospital is now accepting patients. Dr. Pritchard appreciates the well wishes sent to him during his incapacitation.

After that chore was complete, she drove him to Bangor to see his wife. The roads had been well plowed and the trip was uneventful. Before turning into the drive, Albert warned Adele, "This is a horrid place." She believed him at the first sight of the ghastly institution. It consisted of a group of massive four story red brick buildings in need of a good scrubbing. A grayish moss covered the walls, which made the buildings seem infected with a hideous disease. She was soon to learn that they were. Large room height windows invited the light into the building, but the thick translucent panes within them forbade the viewing of God's wonders to those inside. A grid of black iron bars covered each one. Adele imagined that they cast thin shadows on the walls of the rooms they guarded.

As they parked the car, Albert suggested, "Maybe you should wait in the lobby and let me see her first." Adele's voice failed her, so she simply nodded in agreement. As soon as she opened the car door, she heard the cries of the minions of hell. Wild animals howled from within the walls. Demons screamed to be released from their bonds. And Satan himself laughed horribly at their pain. Albert and Adele approached twin forbidden wood doors. For a brief moment Adele thought of Dorothy approaching the domain of the wizard. The doors looked to her to be twelve inches thick or more. When Albert turned the knob and pulled the immense door towards him, she found no relief to learn it was only about four. The audible assault only increased as they entered. She felt pity for Albert for being here before and awed at his strength to return voluntarily. It felt like a lifetime that she waited for him to see Isabelle, and while she waited she conversed with a God that she had not spoken with since her childhood days on Gray Island.

If you carefully dig up a lupine from the wild, plant it in your yard in fertile soil with plenty of sunlight, provide it with water, and remove the weeds from around it that would choke out its life, then it will blossom. And it will continue to blossom and spread, year after year for all to enjoy. Take that same lupine and snatch it up by the roots, and stick it in your ash bucket in the cellar, and it will wither and rot to a slime that no man will touch. And, eventually, it will evolve into a hard and brittle stick. For the first time since she met her, Adele felt sorry for Mrs. Dr. Albert Pritchard.

Adele had her head bowed and eyes closed when Albert came down the hall. He leaned over and touched her shoulder. She jumped up and gave a little cry, almost knocking him off his crutches. As they shut the door to the asylum, they could still hear the moans and wails of the mentally ill. Even in their car as they drove away, they could hear them in their minds. They rode in silence, either because the absence of sound was a peace they needed or because they just didn't know what to say. Albert broke the silence.

"You were praying in there. I saw your lips moving. I thought you were an agnostic."

"I guess it's true that there are no atheists in the foxholes," she replied.

"Were you praying for her physical salvation or my mortal soul?"

"I was praying for all of us," she admitted. "Although I don't know if it'll do any good. Maybe He listens, maybe He doesn't. I'm just to a point in my life where I need to believe in something." This was it. She was going to tell him about Harry. She had to be strong. She looked over and saw him staring out the passenger window. "Albert...."

"Adele, I've done a horrible thing. I addicted my wife to drugs and drove her crazy." She slammed on the brakes and pulled the sliding car to a stop right in the middle of the road. Albert assumed his recently learned position, one hand on the dashboard, one hand on the armrest.

"I don't presume to lecture you," she began. "I haven't the wisdom or the right. But, I will tell you what I think. I don't care what Livingston says. I don't care what those fools say at the county hospital. I don't care what's being whispered around town in little gossipy circles. You did what you've always done. You tried to help somebody who desperately needed help. True. You were not successful. This time…. the best laid plans of mice and men, Albert," she quoted from a book she sneaked off his shelf one night. "You can't let one failure destroy a lifetime of successes. Look around. The healing hands of Albert Pritchard have touched half the lives in this county. You've got to stop torturing yourself. You've got to stop. And if you can't, you will keep it to yourself. I will no longer allow you to denounce, in my presence, a man whom I hold in such high esteem." And with her speech concluded, she started to cry. Albert reached over and took her face in his hands, and kissed her on the forehead.

"You drive like a maniac."

Adele put the car in gear and pulled off slowly. Albert pondered her lecture on the way home. He brought to her attention the part about the whispers about town. He had heard them in the hospital, but in his misery, he ignored them.

"Right or wrong, Adele, a patient must have faith in their physician. Faith in your doctor is a vital part of the healing process."

120

When they reached the county line, he had her retrace the route they had taken earlier. He removed the fliers he had posted and wrote on the back of each one.

Albert Pritchard, M.D. regrets to inform his former patients that, due to health reasons, he is retiring from the practice of medicine. He thanks all for their patronage and wishes all well. Patient records will be available upon request for a period of one year.

For the second time since they left the hospital, Adele cried.

Chapter Fourteen

Deciding that the previous week's stress was too much, Adele insisted that Albert take it easy. After tucking him snugly onto the sofa, as he whined and complained about her making a fuss, Adele lit the home fire and left some logs by the hearth.

"Have Millie load it up before she leaves."

"I can do it." He had begun to expect to have the fireplace burning. "I'm no cripple."

"…Have Millie load it up before she goes. I'm off to Colcord's to pick up some groceries."

"My best to Clayton," he called as she left the house. When he heard the Ford pull off, he frantically tried to kick off the afghan. Finally successful, it flew across the room almost landing in the fireplace. He leaped off the sofa and hopped crutch-less to the window and peeked out from around the curtain, not touching it lest he draw her attention. Satisfied he hopped to the den, picked up the receiver off the phone, fumbled it and grabbed it again. He clicked the hook three or four times. "…Vonnie, Albert…yes, yes, and to yours." He was near giddy. "Get me Malcolm Blake."

When Malcolm didn't arrive as soon as he hung up the telephone, Albert began to pace. He bumped his toe three times and let out a stream of profanity on each bump.

"Where is that husband of yours?"

"You just called him, Dr. Pritchard," Millie excused, giggling under her breath. Malcolm finally arrived. Abner Thomas followed right behind him with wood crates in his truck. Two local boys were in the back, trying to keep the load from shifting. Albert met them at the back door. Reminiscent of a teacher in the schoolyard, he began clapping his hands together.

"Hurry up, boys. Hurry up. That girl goes through the grocery faster than any woman alive." And to encourage further speed, "And she drives like a maniac."

The crew moved with record-setting speed. And, before long, Malcolm and Millie Blake and the boys who came to help them were leaving in the Blake's car. Albert was on the porch removing some money from his wallet. He gave it to Abner.

"When you get there, ask for Dr. Livingston. He's a fat little man with a big mouth. He'll direct you from there. And Abner, try not to slap him."

Abner pulled off his hat and clutched it with one hand into his stomach. Scouting around briefly to ensure that no one was looking, he looked eye to eye at his lifelong friend.

"Albert Pritchard," he said. "You're a good man." Then, very uncharacteristic of Maine men, he threw an arm around Albert, and gave him a half pat, half slap on the back. Then he turned and walked off the porch to his appointed task.

Albert stood there puzzled for several minutes, and then entered the house. He heard the familiar honk of Abner's horn and took it as a warning. He half hopped, half ran into the sitting room and assumed his place on the sofa.

Adele pulled open the screen door with the toe of her shoe. Both arms were full of grocery sacks. Leaning into the back door, she turned the knob with the tips of her fingers. She did a quick about face, careful not to lose her load, and bumped the door open with her backside. It was a maneuver she had perfected after strewing groceries over the porch a few times during the experimental stage. She turned into the kitchen and set the groceries on the counter. When she turned back to the parlor to close the door, she called out.

"Albert?"

'Yes, Adele," he said innocently.

"Albert Pritchard!" Albert walked with crutches into his former parlor/office. Adele was tracing the lines of a mahogany dining room table with her fingers. Then she traced the back of one of the six chairs. She eyed the china cabinet in the corner, and the large buffet on the opposing wall. A larger oval mirror hung over the buffet. She had not yet seen the crystal chandelier hung where the examination light used to be.

"Where's your equipment?"

"I sent it off to the asylum." He started to say *as I did my wife*, but decided against it. "It's mahogany. It came all the way from New York. Do you like it?"

She was briefly speechless. "Albert, I think it's the most beautiful furniture I've ever seen."

Albert got his pork roast that night. And they ate it in their new dining room. Adele set at one end, Albert at the other. He saw her looking around the room.

"Is something wrong?" Albert asked from across the table.

"Yes, it's missing something."

"Missing something? He laughed. "What's it missing; King Solomon's throne?"

"No. Excuse me a minute." She got up and ran upstairs.

"Adele?" He asked puzzled.

"Just a second," she called and ran down the stairs and into the den. She took the Hippocratic Oath from behind the desk. Albert put it there the day he got back from the hospital. She removed it from the frame.

"Adele, your supper's getting cold."

"Be there in a minute!" After a few busy minutes she returned to the dining room and hung the frame back in its original home. Its contents had been removed and replaced with a white cloth with black lettering cross stitched into it. It read: *The quality of mercy is never strained. It falls from heaven like the gentle rain.* His heart lightened in his chest and the depression that had plagued him found a release, not a cure, but at least a release. They ate their meal in a happy home.

Chapter Fifteen

That night Adele sat in her room and pondered her future. With Albert settled back into his home and on the road to recovery, her thoughts returned to Harry. The thought of carrying his bastard child did not dissolve the love she had for him. Before Harry she was but a functioning machine. He brought color to her canvas. Like the Michelangelo painting of the hands of God and Adam, Harry had touched her and started her existence. Whatever tomorrow might bring, whatever road she might be forced to travel, she would never regret the night she dragged his bleeding body into the parlor. Nor would she regret taking him up to her grandmother's bed. With a resolve such as she had never felt, she lifted herself out off that same bed and walked over to confront the sarcastic gift she received from Mrs. Avery.

"Little fellow, you will have no more secrets to whisper about me."

Albert and Adele had their breakfast the next morning in the kitchen. One doesn't have breakfast in the dining room, regardless of how new it may be. Afterward, she planted him on the sofa, and built a fire. He was lying back comfortably reading *Candide*. She felt the toes that protruded from his cast and slipped her hand under it and felt the heel.

"I suspected as much," she accused. She got no response. "You've been walking on your cast."

He stayed with his book. "You know that Pangloss was a pompous ass." She covered his legs and feet with an afghan and tucked him in.

"Maybe he should get a job at the hospital." She smiled at her own wit, left the room, and closed the door leading to the den behind her. He peered over his glasses and lifted his casted leg and inspected the heel. It was flattening out. He dropped his leg, leaving it uncovered and shrugged his shoulders. He then read on to see what other disasters would befall Candide.

Millie was starting the breakfast dishes when Adele entered the kitchen. She pulled the string of the apron Millie was wearing, untying it, and pulled it out from around the cook's waist. Millie turned in surprise as Adele was tying the apron around her own waist.

"Miss Abbott?"

"Millie, you work so hard around here. Go home and let me finish the dishes."

"Oh, you don't have to do that. It's my job."

"To be honest with you, Millie, I need to talk to Dr. Pritchard and I think it's best that we be alone."

Millie leaned into Adele's face. "You gonna tell him about Harry Wallace?"

"I'm going to tell him about Harry Wallace."

Still face to face with Adele, Millie called out. "I'll be going now, Dr. Pritchard. See you this evening." She smiled at Adele and whispered, "I'll be praying for you." With that she bolted out the door.

"My best to Malcolm," Albert called from the sitting room. But, by that time, Millie was halfway down the drive. Adele finished the dishes, removed the apron, and folded it neatly. She placed it on the counter and smoothed it flat. She took a deep breath and released it. Her heart started to pound and she could hear it in her ears. She started out of the kitchen, balked, and thought about sitting down at the kitchen table, just to get a grip on what she was going to say.

"Now or never," she said. She went into the den and took the small chair from the desk. Carrying it into the sitting room, she placed it by the sofa and sat in it. Closeness was needed. And should he choose to strike her, she wanted it over with quickly. "Albert, we need to talk."

"I'm reading," he said, trying to avoid a lecture about his cast.

"It's important. I need to tell you something." When he looked up at her face, he could tell it was, indeed, important. He closed his book and removed his glasses. He stowed them in a hard-shelled, leather covered case. He placed them and his book on the side table Adele had brought in for his convenience. Pushing up with his elbows, he made himself comfortable. By her expression, this could take awhile.

It is better to heed the rebuke of a wise man than to listen to the songs of fools. Adele had listened to the songs of fools many times before. People who want something from you or feel indebted to you will tell you what they think you want to hear. Now she must listen to the rebuke. And however it might go, she was going to heed it. She related the whole story, from Harry's abdominal wound to her morning sickness. She left nothing out; sugar coated no part of it, and made no omissions. She intended to end it with *I'll pack my things if you wish*, but decided that was a shameful way to fish for sympathy. She didn't want to influence his reaction, one way or the other. She just laid it out and, as they say, let the chips fall where they may. She looked him square in his eye during the whole telling. She never flinched and neither did he. When she was through, she dropped her head; perhaps out of shame, perhaps out of exhaustion.

Albert did not respond at first. He was reflecting. He remembered a young girl, amazed by a flushing toilet, who tried to connive, even blackmail her way into his home. He looked back on his decision to try to redeem a child of the sardine factory, as opposed to aborting yet another one. He reminisced watching her become a caring, intelligent, and strong woman. He recalled how she lifted him out of his despair, stuck by him when others abandoned him, and carried him through the muck in her arms. And in his reflection, love swelled his heart and pride swelled his head. He tried to think of something profound to say, but nothing came to him. So, he did the next best thing. He made light of it.

"You were always a studious child, Adele. But I have to ask. Have you ever drunk any liquor in my house?"

She lifted her head. "What? Albert, you know I don't drink alcohol."

"Well hell, girl. Two out of three's not that bad."

The relief made her so dizzy that she thought she'd fall out of the chair. The guilt weighed so heavy on her that she thought she'd sink into it. In desperation, she threw up her hands. "I deceived you. You've been so good to me. I feel so bad. I'm a horrible person."

He leaned towards her and volleyed her own words back at her. "I will not allow you to denounce, in my presence, a woman whom I hold in such high esteem."

She smiled. He reached over and touched her belly. "Imagine, a baby in this house. I never thought I'd live to see the day." He saw she was going to cry. "Now, if you don't mind…" He picked up his book and put on his glasses. "…Candide is about to have half of his ass bit off."

Chapter Sixteen

Albert had begun to pay Malcolm to drive him to Bangor to see Isabelle. Adele had nightmares after her first visit that left her screaming into consciousness. She protested not taking him. She felt it was her responsibility. But Albert stood his ground, reasoning to her that he could not stand to lose any more sleep. Adele conceded and tried to conceal her relief by telling Albert that he was stubborn as a goat.

On one such visit he was gone much longer than she felt it should take. Worried, she went out on the porch to wait for him. Albert arrived, to her relief, and she went to the car and asked it everything was all right. He assured her that it was, and headed to the porch. She followed and asked how Isabelle was doing.

"About the same," he said going into the house. Adele followed him in and he sat at the dining room table. He asked her to have a seat. As she sat, he took her by the hands.

"Adele," he said, "do you trust me?"

"Of course I do," she answered somewhat insulted.

"If I asked you to do something that was a little...well, let's say bizarre, would you do it?"

Adele lifted her eyebrows. "How bizarre?"

He launched into a speech about life in rural Maine and the difficulties of life for illegitimate children. It was nothing she didn't know or hadn't dwelt on nights in her bedroom.

"I'm not having an abortion!"

"I wouldn't let you."

"I'm not giving up Harry's baby for adoption!"

"No one is going to adopt my grandson."

She smiled and squeezed his hands. "Then, what?"

"Think of those three options; abortion, adoption, being called a bastard, what if there was another way? What if we had a fourth option?"

"Go on", she instructed.

"Do you trust me?"

"Yes, I trust you."

"Good, go upstairs and put on your uniform. Fix your hair."

"Albert?"

"Do...you...trust...me?" At first, she thought he had lost his mind. He'd caught something at the insane asylum. But the sincerity in his face convinced her, and she went upstairs and did what he had asked.

Albert had her drive him to the Jonasport 2nd Congregational Church. On the way he instructed her. "Don't ask any questions. This needs to go fast. There won't be time for explanations. When you are asked a question, you'll know what to say."

As they entered the vestibule Adele paused. Reverend McIntosh was behind the altar wearing his vestment. A photographer was setting up his tripod and camera in the aisle. Sheriff Farnham and Miss Jonas were sitting in the front pew. Next to Miss Jonas was a man Adele did not recognize. When he stood up and faced her she almost ran out the door, but Albert braced her.

"Come on, dear," Miss Jonas called. "Don't dawdle."

Albert gave her a little push to get her going and then sat in the last pew. When she got closer, she recognized the man she thought she didn't know. It was Thomas Avery. But he was clean and clean-shaven. And he was sober. But stranger yet, he was wearing the clothing of a merchant sailor. His hair had been cropped off and bleached out. He looked as though he had received a shock and his hair whitened over night.

"Good evening, Nurse Abbott," a healthier Mr. Avery said.

"Good evening, Mr. Avery. You're looking…. good."

"I feel good, ma'am. I ain't had a drink in a coon's age. And Mr. Drucker just made me foreman at the yard. My boys are growing tall and strong. And it's all thanks to you, ma'am."

"And I suppose the Lord had nothing to do with it", admonished the Reverend.

"And the Lord," Mr. Avery corrected himself.

"Enough chit-chat," Miss Jonas demanded. She reached into her oversized handbag and produced a veil she had made earlier that day. It was just after the good doctor had called her and she stuck herself with the needle twice in her haste to get it done. She placed the bridal crown on Adele's head. She fussed with it a little, and then she positioned Mr. Avery and Adele. The photographer plied his trade.

"Okay ma'am, could you turn your body just a little to the right... more...good. Hold that pose." Mr. Avery turned also, and Miss Jonas pushed his head back with the tip of her cane. His face could not be in the picture. "Now ho-o-ld!" An explosion erupted from his flash pan. The light left Adele seeing white with bits of yellow jumping around in her vision. It had just cleared when the photographer said, "One more just in case....sm-ile and ho-o-o-ld!"

As he laid his plates in his case and started to dismantle his equipment, the reverend approached the podium and started to immediately speak.

"Dearly beloved, we are gathered together today in the presence of God and all these witnesses to join together Harry...." He looked to Adele for his next line.

"Andrew," Adele injected.

"...to join Harry Andrew Wallace and Adele Susannah Abbott in the bonds of holy matrimony." In light of the situation the Reverend decided he would just get to the important parts. "Do you Harry take Adele as your lawfully wedded wife?"

After a poke in the ribs from Miss Jonas' cane, Mr. Avery threw out his answer. "I do!"

The reverend continued with the most rapid ceremony ever perform in the small white chapel. "Do you Adele take Harry as your lawfully wedded husband?"

Adele closed her eyes. She was not in the chapel. She was aboard the *Sovereign State*. Harry was by her side and the ships chaplain was standing before them. Her heart sent the word to her brain, which gave instruction to her mouth to release the truest statement she ever made. "I do."

"Who stands today to give this bride away?"

Sheriff Farnham stood and cleared his throat. "Her guardian, Dr. Albert Pritchard, who is currently incapacitated in the Soctomah County Hospital, gives the bride away. I stand in his stead and relay his consent."

The reverend rolled his eyes. "By the power vested in me by the State of Maine and the Lord our God, I now pronounce you man and wife. And may God have mercy on your souls". His last sentence was accompanied by a turning head, casting eyes at all of the wedding party. Then he snapped his Bible closed, removed his vestment, and dropped it in a chair. He hurried up the aisle putting on his coat. As he approached the last pew, Albert held up an envelope containing the fees for ten ceremonies between two fingers. The reverend snatched it like the brass ring on a merry-go-round. Before leaving the church, he turned his head and blurted out, "What God had joined together, let no man put asunder." And as he went through the door, "You may kiss the bride." And he was gone.

Mr. Avery turned towards Adele, and Miss Jonas, always-on guard, warned, "You do, Tommy Avery, and I'll cane you!" All the accomplices broke into laughter and poor Mr. Avery turned red in the face. When Adele leaned over and kissed her groom on the forehead, his redness increased a shade.

Sheriff Farnham sealed the deal on his first and last illegal activity. "All right, let's get down to business." He picked up his clipboard off of the pew he was sitting on. He pulled a loaded fountain pen from his shirt pocket and gave it to Tommy. "Sign here, Harry A Wallace." Tommy scratched out the name. He gave back the pen. The sheriff checked the signature, nodded and held it before Adele. "Now you Mrs. Wallace, sign your maiden name please." Adele signed and the sheriff handed her the license. Then, he handed her a marriage certificate already signed by the Reverend. Adele studied both. She noticed the license was dated two weeks before Harry shipped out and the certificate dated the day before she took him to the docks. According to the documents they got married the day he asked her, the day she got pregnant.

"How did you do it?" Adele asked in amazement.

"Dr. Pritchard delivered the town clerk's children," Miss Jonas said.

Albert called out from his backseat, "One was a breach!"

Chapter Seventeen

Life in the white two-story colonial perched on the banks of the Penobscot River progressed at a pace dictated by the ever-changing Maine weather. The long cold winter sent most people indoors except when necessity forced them out of the house. Socializing was kept at a minimum, and people kept up with each other during trips to the stores and Sunday meetings at church. This is how the word of Adele's short marriage and Harry's death got out. Albert and Adele's closest associates were the vehicles for the information. Millie planted the seed at Colcord's Grocery. *That poor Adele widowed so soon after her wedding. What? You didn't know she was married?* Mrs. Thomas watered the growing sapling. *Well, I wasn't there. I understand it was a small affair. They say she didn't make a big to do about it, what with Albert being laid up and his wife being sent away.* And Malcolm and Abner set the tone by starting to refer to her at the gas station and barbershop as the widow Wallace. Whirlwind marriages in a seafaring town were not uncommon. And in coastal New England, widows of sailors were as numerous as lobster traps. By spring, people who were not at the wedding related to their friends what a beautiful bride she had made. And others who never met Harry recalled what a fine young man he was. Soon the whole affair was replaced by the next family's troubles, and Adele and Albert got on with their lives.

Albert had his cast removed. It left him with a permanent limp and an aching pain on cold nights that he tried to knead out with his hands. He walked with a cane. It was a sturdy piece of oak with a knob cut into the top for gripping and intricate carvings that ran down the length of it for aesthetic appeal. It was a present from Jack Drucker. When he presented it, he told the story that it was made by one of his skilled artisans who gave it to him as a token of the esteem that his entire crew held for him. Truth was he confiscated it from a young employee who Jack knew was working on it while he was supposed to be running the plank planer. The boy gave it up without protest but later complained to his buddies over beers, "The old bastard waited until I finished the damn thing!" One or two of his buddies slapped him on the back and the whole bar roared. Jack attached the brass tip himself before giving it to Albert.

A noticeable limp was the second casualty of Albert's accident. He never drove a car again. With the exception of his trips to see Isabelle, Adele became his chauffeur. But riding in her rickety Ford gave him the jitters. He felt the potholes in the county road and Adele's rum runner driving had surely destroyed the undercarriage of the car. He could almost hear the bolts holding the whole thing together breaking or backing out as he rode in it.

His fears caused him to send Adele to Bangor to buy a new car and trade in the old one, or "push the damn thing into the Penobscot." She amended his original plan to go with her. He had bought automobiles before and knew a few things about the subject. She pleaded with him not to go as she wanted to pick it out herself and she knew how men were when it came to machines. He wouldn't be able to help himself from taking over. He could have sworn she had stomped her foot. So, he gave in knowing in his heart that she was much sharper at business than he was. Adele would probably leave the poor dealer crying at his desk.

And she nearly did. She arrived at the automobile dealership and advised the proprietor that she wanted to trade her Ford in on a newer model. The first thing he asked was the whereabouts of her husband.

"He was lost at sea," she informed him, "aboard the *Sovereign State*."

He bowed his head and sadly offered his condolences. He remembered reading about it in the paper, dreadful, simply dreadful. He quickly removed that mask and donned a business face to inspect her car. He kicked the tires and rocked the fenders as he walked around the Ford that had done her so well. He glanced under the chassis and checked under the hood. All the while he was popping his tongue against the roof of his mouth and mumbling about women being hard on cars and the apparent lack of maintenance. When he had come full circle, he made her a paltry offer and, shaking his head, added he could probably sell it for parts.

"I can get twice that from any farmer in town". She was opening the car door to leave as she spoke.

He grabbed the door. "Whoa! Wait a minute little lady. That's just my first offer. This whole business is all about dickering."

"Do not call me little lady," she said, recalling the words of Tibias Anderson. "My name is Mrs. Wallace." The word Wallace almost got caught in her throat.

"Of course, ma'am, of course, why don't we look at some of our fine automobiles?" He tried to pitch his most expensive model.

"Now this here is the prize of Pierce Arrow; the 1928 Series 81. It's made with a new technology called sheet metal. Look at the smoothness, like it was poured into existence. And you know, since the Taft Administration, Pierce Arrows have been the car of the White House."

"How much is it?"

"And the Pierce family knows manufacturing. Why, from birdcages to bicycles, this family's products have been in American homes for over a century."

"How much is it?" He could see she was interested in only the bottom line.

"I can let you have it for four thousand and forty-five dollars. That's a good price for the car of presidents." Adele liked the red color and little archer on the radiator cap, but she thought the crest of the Pierce family on the grill was a little too much. And it was a lot too much money for a car. She chose the 1928 Studebaker Tourer. She sat inside of it just to get the feel. She knew the white color would be hard to keep clean in the spring mud season. But she fell in love with it almost as fast as she did Harry. And she told the story for years to come how Studerbaker bought the Pierce Arrow Company that same year, putting her in the car that was produced by the company that provided cars to the president for half the price. They went into the office and when she had dickered to her satisfaction, she sat at his desk to seal the deal. She produced a crisp new marriage certificate as proof of identification. She felt he studied it a little long. She felt he was getting suspicious. When he handed it back to her and started to draw up the necessary paperwork, she felt more at ease. She signed the sales agreement at the bottom, Mrs. Harry Wallace. It was the first time, and she became that woman in heart and deed on that day.

"Okay, Mrs. Wallace, let's talk about payments." Adele picked up her handbag off the floor and placed it in her lap. She drew out an envelope and set it on the desk.

"It's all there." She knew at the bank how much she was willing to spend. The broker emptied the contents and counted it. Without speaking he took a receipt book out of a drawer in his desk and filled it out. He handed Adele the receipt and title.

Adele thanked him and took her new car home. The broker went to the window and watched her pull off. Then heading back in his office, he put the money into his safe. He flopped down at his desk and leaned back. He glanced at the bottom drawer of his desk and took a loud deep breath. Reaching into the drawer, he retrieved a pewter flask, uncapped it, and poured the contents down his throat. "Either I'm getting dumber, or their getting smarter." He took another swig.

Chapter Eighteen

Winter had come to Jonasport and the first snow had been cleared. Adele was looking out of the kitchen window, watching swirls of snow mist making their way down the driveway. She would watch one until it landed on the small drift the wind had created down by the road. Then, she would look back up and follow another as it started its journey. Her entertainment ended when Abner Thomas drove his truck into the yard, flattening the snowdrifts and dissipating the snow swirls as he made his way up to the house.

"The Thomas' are here", she called out to Albert.

"Hurray!" His feigned enthusiasm halted her as she made her way to the back door. She turned and went into the den, where he was sitting at his desk.

"Albert, I know you don't agree, but Mrs. Thomas asked me to go and I have to keep my word. Besides, I agree with her that my child should be brought up understanding the word of the Lord. I need to learn it before I teach it."

"Then read the Bible. I can't see you sitting still for an hour-long lecture from that fast talking, bible-thumping fool. I'll wage that you won't make it through the first ten minutes. But don't listen to me. You never do."

There was a knock on the back door. Adele leaned over and kissed Albert on the top on his head. "Well", she said. "It seems foolish to start now. I'll get the door." Albert rose and followed her to meet the Thomas'. The plan had already been laid. Adele was going to church with Mrs. Thomas, and Albert was to spend his Sunday morning playing chess with Abner. As soon as the Thomas' came through the door, Albert paid his respects to Mrs. Thomas and hurried his old friend into the den.

"You ready to go, dear? You look lovely." Mrs. Thomas always thought Adele looked lovely.

"Almost", Adele said. She was waiting for Albert's final remark.

"Yes, go and get your soul saved, you heathen", he called from the den.

Adele slipped on her gloves. "Now I'm ready."

The congregation had already gathered in the church when Mrs. Thomas and Adele arrived. Mr. and Mrs. Drucker had come earlier to deliver Miss Jonas, who played organ and piano every Sunday. Miss Jonas was seated at the piano and Jack Drucker was seated in the deacon's chair opposite the Reverend. People had taken their usually pews and were looking through their church bulletin or chatting with their neighbors. The Reverend

McIntosh was sitting in his chair behind the pulpit readying his self for this week's sermon. He noticed people gathering around Adele and Mrs. Thomas. Some simply waved to them from where they sat. Most left their pews and came over to greet them. There were very few in the church whose lives Adele had not touched in one manner or the other. They were delighted to finally see their angel of mercy in the house of God. Mrs. Thomas was receiving accolades for being the vehicle of Adele's delivery. The interaction disturbed the good reverend. As he considered himself the Shepard of this flock, he did not like to see the apparent influence this unholy woman appeared to have over his congregation. *It is not by good deeds that one enters the kingdom of heaven,* he assured himself.

Miss Jonas, seated at the piano, began to play *Church in the Wildwood*, as she did every Sunday, to announce the beginning of the service. Reverend McIntosh reached over and took his Bible from the pulpit. He frantically began searching for the passages he needed as the church came to order. He was still searching when the song ended and all eyes turned to the minister. Finding the passage he needed, he slipped a bookmark between the pages and slapped the book shut. He nodded to the deacon.

Jack Drucker rose and approached the pulpit to deliver that week's announcements. "Good morning", he offered.

"Good morning!" came the unified response. Adele remained silent; not knowing the reply would be forthcoming. She turned her head towards Mrs. Thomas and shrugged her shoulders. Mrs. Thomas gave her an understanding nod and a smile.

"There will be a rehearsal of the church play at the Community Center on Tuesday. Miss Jonas tells me that everyone is expected at six o'clock sharp." He paused and read silently. "Oh yes, the Woman's Auxiliary will be providing refreshments immediately following the evening's rehearsal." He shuffled his pages and cleared his throat. "At last week's deacon's meeting, it was noted that only two boys have signed up to shovel out the shut-ins this winter. We have six homes on our list and need a couple of more volunteers. Now we expect some of you strapping young lads to step forward and do your civic duty". That said, he took his seat and nodded to Reverend McIntosh. The Reverend rose and took his place at the pulpit.

"Good people of Jonasport, I welcome you into the House of Jehovah. If the ushers will come forward we will accept your weekly tithe. Please remember that we are still quite short on our goal for the new boiler. Give with your heart". Miss Jonas had switched to the organ and was quietly playing *Shall We Gather at the River*. Adele had her purse opened when the usher passed the collection basket down her row. But she waited to withdraw any monies until she saw Mrs. Thomas pull a dime from her purse. Adele took out her own dime and placed it in the basket. Mrs. Thomas nodded and smiled. Adele was beginning to enjoy herself.

Reverend McIntosh accepted the baskets from the ushers, returned to the pulpit and placed the baskets underneath it. He took a step back and grasped the pulpit with both hands. He slowly bowed his head and closed his eyes. He raised his head and spoke with eyes closed. "Lord, be with me, your humble servant, as I use Your Divine Word to drive-e-e Satan from our midst". He opened his eyes and scanned the congregation. "If you please, I feel I must vary from the sermon I prepared for today. I had intended to speak about the wages of sin, in general, but something has come to my attention that *must* be addressed. A specific sin has made its way into the heart of a certain member of our flock, and the apparent acceptance of this sinner is jeopardizing the very fabric of our community." He paused and scanned the faces in the church. All eyes were on him and, feeling comfortable with his position, he continued. "Miss Jonas, since I'm in a changing mood, let us sing number 242 instead of the hymn we decided on." Miss Jonas and the congregation turned to *Onward Christian Soldier* in their hymnals. "Please rise."

Adele Wallace had a wonderful speaking voice. She read with such elegance that she had been asked to be narrator of the annual performance of *The Peabody Pew.* But the woman could not carry a tune in a bucket. That did not deter her and she belted the song out as best she could. When the last stanza was sung and Adele resumed her seat in the pew, she, again, looked over to Mrs. Thomas and shrugged her shoulders. Mrs. Thomas patted Adele's hand and whispered. "It says we should *make a joyful noise into the Lord.* It doesn't say we have to be on key." Adele smiled, but her smile disappeared when the reverend started his sermon.

"I will be reading from the book of Proverbs, Chapter Five, starting with Verse Three." The congregation dutifully began searching for the verse. He had commenced reading before most found their place. *"For the lips of a strange woman drop as a honeycomb, and her mouth is smoother than oil. But her end is bitter as wormwood, sharp as a two-edged sword. Her feet go down to death; her steps take hold of hell. Lest thou shouldest ponder the path of her life, her ways are movable, that thou canst not know them. Hear me now, O ye children, and depart not from the words of my mouth. Remove thy way far from her, and come not nigh the door of her home."* Adele looked up from her Bible and, at first, thought he was looking directly at her. Then

147

she realized that his eyes were attempting to address Mrs. Thomas. Surely, he wasn't accusing Mrs. Thomas of adultery. Suddenly, his intention struck her. He wasn't accusing Mrs. Thomas of adultery. He was warning her not to *come not nigh the door* of the Pritchard home. He was accusing Adele of adultery. Her face reddened and she closed her Bible and curled her fingers into her hands until her fingernails dug into the skin of her palms. The inquisition continued. *Lest thou give thine honour unto others, and thine years to the cruel. Lest strangers be filled with thy wealth, and thy labours be in the house of a stranger. And thou mourn at the last, when thy flesh and thy body are consumed, and say, how have I hated instruction, and my heart despised reproof. And have not obeyed the voice of my teachers."* He looked at Adele who was glaring at him. He lost his place in his Bible. "Um…yes, *obeyed the voice of my teachers, nor inclined mine ear to them that instructed me! I was almost in all evil in the midst of the congregation and assembly.* He closed his Bible and, again, scanned the faces in the church. He skipped over Adele. "Adultery! The deadly sin! It affects not only the sinner, but also the innocent around them. Yea even more damnable than the woman who takes another's husband is the woman who takes the husband of a woman that welcomed the sinner into her home. Bless the poor woman who raised the sinner as though she came from her own womb and was rewarded by being driven from her house. How damnable it is in the eyes of God to steal a woman's husband and her home." Adele gathered her gloves and coat. Albert was wrong. She lasted ten minutes, but not much more. Mrs. Thomas reached over and touched her arm.

"Don't give him the satisfaction, dear", she whispered. Adele settled back into her seat. She laid her coat on the pew next to her. The Reverend watched her as she did.

Reverend McIntosh took up his Bible and held it in his open palm. He laid his finger on the spot where he had stopped reading. Taking a step back, he stepped out from behind the pulpit and forward to the edge of the altar. "The Lord is telling you right here in Proverbs Five…" he tapped the book with his finger, "to steer clear of this sort of woman." He took in a deep breath and released it. "Now we know that there are many in our community that knows not of these things. Living under the blanket of this Holy House such sins are foreign to them. But some of the worldlier, more experienced of you know of what I speak. It is your responsibility to shun the wicked and drive them from our midst, unless they fall to their knees in shame and pay retribution to the community that has been soiled by their deeds and desires." He looked at Adele. He had expected to see her with her head down. When he met her eyes he shook where he stood. Speech failed him. It was not a look of hatred or, even, anger. It was not a threat. It was a dare. He fell silent. The mere thought of accepting her challenge made his heart quiver. He looked to his Bible, but had lost his place. A quiet murmur began to make its way around the chapel. It started somewhere in the back right corner. Then, the sound was heard down front close to where Miss Jonas was sitting by the piano. The sound began to amplify throughout the church. It was the sound of voices whispering to each other. He began to notice that people were shaking their heads. He decided to retreat. Perhaps, this was not the time. He closed the book and placed it under his arm. He returned to the pulpit where he felt more at ease. He lifted his left hand into the air and announced, "But lo, He is a forgiving God. It is never too late to change. If any of you feel the need for salvation on this day, come forth as Miss Jonas plays Number 78, *Just As I Am.* Please rise and sing." When the song was over and no one came forth to be saved, the Reverend made one last announcement. "I won't be able to greet you at the door today as I have a pressing engagement. The deacon will offer the benediction. Go with God." He exited the church through the back door as Jack rose to bless the congregation. With the service dismissed and the worshipers prepared to leave, Mrs. Thomas turned to Adele.

"Dear, don't…" Adele shook her head from side to side.

"It's fine. I can only concern myself with sins I've actually committed. I have no time to worry about the imagination of others." She rose, put on her coat and followed Mrs. Thomas out of the row and up the aisle. As people approached, Adele took charge of the conversation. "Oh, Mrs. Landry, how's your bursitis?" "Mr. Johnson, you're boys are growing tall." She was determined not to let her neighbors feel uncomfortable for her.

On the way home, Mrs. Thomas offered an excuse. "You know, we don't get to choose the preacher?"

"You don't?"

"No, the church sends them. When Pastor Green died, we lost a great minister. This young man…I just don't know."

"He won't last."

When they arrived at the Pritchard house, Albert and Abner were having a can of sardines and soda crackers for lunch. Adele was wearing her poker face, but when the men saw Mrs. Thomas, they knew that things had not gone well. Albert decided it best not to question Adele, and she never spoke of the incident. Albert would later find out from Abner, but he, too, never spoke of it except to ask that night. "Do you think you'll go back to church?"

"Someday", she said.

When spring came to Maine, the snow that had gathered in the hills turned to water and the runoff had brought the brook out behind the Pritchard house to near flood conditions. One low spot had broken through and created a stream of water that flowed from the brook, past the back of the house and followed a diagonal line across the driveway on its migration to the bay. By the time the brook returned to its normal level, and the stream it created in the Pritchard yard had dried up, Adele was in the last trimester of her pregnancy.

Dr. Pritchard was giving her yet another prenatal examination. Knowing that she would be his last patient, or rather his last adult patient, he had taken to examining her with a frequency that she began to find annoying. Yet, she didn't protest. It gave him something to do to occupy his empty time and she wanted to do whatever she could to ensure a trouble-free delivery and, more important, a healthy outcome for the child growing within her. He had completed his measuring, poking, and feeling and asked the last of his series of questions. He had nodded or raised his eyebrows at the various answers she provided. And, he completed his exam with his usual, "Well, so far, so good. We'll have another look next week." He was washing his hands when Malcolm arrived in his dump truck filled with dirt and pulling his tractor to repair the damage to the driveway. Albert went out to greet his hired man.

"Thank God," he said as Malcolm was inspecting the drive and formulating a plan. "She has to come to a complete stop and creep over that gully wash. And you know how she hates to stop for anything."

Malcolm knew, and knowing went right to work on it. First he filled the wash out with gravel. He used his tractor to unearth large rocks and small boulders that had been pushed to the surface by frost. Then, he filled the holes left behind. Satisfied with the base of the drive, he dragged his tractor's blade up and down the length of the driveway until he was satisfied with the grade. He left a slight cant towards the bay to ensure an even runoff of the summer's rain. Pleased with the job he had done on the driveway, he set about to repair the damage that Adele's tires had left in the front lawn. He filled the ruts with a shovel and ran his tractor tires over them to compact the earth. He threw out grass seed in the scars left on the lawn, covered the bare ground with hay to assist in germination and prevent erosion. Lastly, he wet the whole area down and advised Adele to keep it wet whenever God chose not to. It was dark by the time he loaded his tractor. Albert paid him in cash, a slap on the back, and praise for his work that every man needs.

Adele and Albert were pleased with their new driveway, but not as much as the neighborhood children. They would ride down the road on their bicycles and veer into the drive, make a loop behind Adele's car and race off back out to horny corner. They did this partially because it was a place to go, but mainly because they admired the smoothness of the driveway compared to that of the pothole filled town road that had yet to be repaired. Albert and Adele didn't try to shoo them away out of fear they might run into the car or fall off their bikes. They didn't even mind the god-awful racket the kids

152

made. The truth be told, they enjoyed their laughter and squeals as they swooped in and raced out. They were enjoying such an event one evening after having supper in the dining room. Adele was in her rocker starting a new sampler, and Albert was settling into his with *The Adventures of Tom Sawyer*, by Mark Twain, whom he insisted on calling Samuel Clemens.

"It's just his pen name," Adele said when he started his tirade.

"Well, it's stupid. I can't for the life of me understand why a body wouldn't use their own name." Adele shifted her eyes in his direction, and catching them, it came to him what he had just said. The redness in his face was enough to show Adele that he realized his error.

Adele's cross-stitched sampler hanging in the dining room was such a success with Albert that she decided to make more of them. She had perfected her *H*, and had started to add little illustrations. They were beginning to fill the walls of their home, and were beginning to annoy Albert. "It's like living inside of *Poor Richard's Almanac*", he told Abner. So Adele started to hand them out to friends and neighbors. She was currently working on one for Mr. Avery, who wanted to hang it on the wall of his office at the lumberyard. She only consented after he assured her that neither lady nor child ever entered the office. He wanted it to read *don't let your bulldog mouth overrun your poodle dog behind.* She had completed the saying and the bulldog on the left side. She was putting the finishing touches on the little poodle on the right when two boys and a girl came screaming in on their bicycles. As the girl was in the middle of her turnaround she called out to the porch, "Hello Dr. Pritchard, hello Mrs. Wallace!" She lifted a hand off the handlebars to wave and almost crashed into the porch. She quickly grabbed a hold of the grip, made a wobbly recovery, and followed the boys down the drive. Albert and Adele returned her greeting to the back of her head.

Still looking down the drive, Albert remarked, "She takes me to mind of you the first day you climbed over these steps."

"Does she now?"

"Well, I guess she's a little younger," he said leading to something.

Adele was removing the sampler to stretch the cloth. "Uh-huh."

"How old were you, Adele, when your mother passed on, fourteen… fifteen?"

Honesty was now her trademark. She turned to Albert. "I was twelve."

"Really, as I recall, you were tall for your age."

"I was," she said returning to her craft.

"That would put your birth at what? 1910?"

"1908," she corrected. "Did you forget your math?"

"Your Harry was about your age, wasn't he?"

She turned to him. "We were exactly the same age, Albert. What are you getting at?"

"Nothing," he defended.

"I know you, Albert Pritchard. You're up to something."

He expounded on his defense. "Oh, for the love of God, woman, can't a body make conversation anymore without going before the judge?"

"I'm sorry. I don't mean to be so testy."

"That's all right," he said returning to his book. "It's the hormones."

Chapter Nineteen

Miss Abigail Leola Jonas, matriarch of the town of Jonasport and direct descendent of its founder, did not survive the winter. She was interned until the thaw at the Jenkins and Smith Funeral Home and buried in the spring. The entire town and half of the county attended the service at the cemetery. Located across the highway from the 2nd Congregational Church, the cemetery lay on the banks of the Penobscot and had been there since before there was a highway. It contained the remains of Jonasport's ancestry with plots dating back into the 1700s.

Adele was the crutch that held Thomas Avery up as he openly wept throughout the service. His two stepsons stood behind them shuffling their feet and gazing about here and there. They were a little disturbed and a lot embarrassed by their stepfather's emotional display. As Miss Jonas was returned to the earth and the remaining members of the Friends of Joshua

Chamberlain sang *Rock of Ages*, Mr. Avery fell to his knees and wailed. Adele let him, and knelt next him, securing him with a warm embrace. When it was all over and she lifted him up, the reverend came walking towards them. He nodded curtly at Adele, but did not speak. He took Mr. Avery's hands and mumbled something about eternal life and God's peaceful shores. He made his departure, passing by Albert and removed the envelope the doctor was holding between two fingers.

The retired doctor and former nurse escorted the recovering alcoholic to his car. When they arrived, Adele informed Mr. Avery that she and Albert didn't see enough of him and his boys. She insisted they come to supper on Sunday as Millie was making venison that her Malcolm had killed and roasted potatoes. (The Avery's came and Mr. Avery came often afterward. The two became good friends, and she became his surrogate sister. It was her plan all along, lest he fall back into the bottle.) As the grieving man loaded his boys into the back seat, he asked Adele to call him Tommy. He related that all his friends called him by that name. When he got behind the wheel she leaned over and said, "Your hair's come back nicely, Tommy." And for the second time in the period of a year, she kissed him on the forehead.

Adele was reminiscing about the funeral as she framed the sampler she had made for Tommy. Malcolm had taken Albert to Bangor to visit Isabelle. So she decided it would be a good time to visit Miss Jonas' grave. She would have to give up driving for a while and felt this might be her last chance to go to the cemetery. She was backing out of the drive when Malcolm pulled in to deposit Albert.

Albert walked up to the car as she was waving to the honking Malcolm.

"Where are you off to?" Albert asked.

"I'm going up to the cemetery to visit Miss Jonas."

"I'll go with you," he offered

"You don't have to."

"You shouldn't be driving by yourself. You'll have my grandchild born in a ditch. I'm going with you." She found him cute when he tried to be forceful.

"Well, alright." She reached the out window and dabbed a yellow spot on his breast pocket. She rubbed the residue between her fingers. "Go change your shirt. I see Malcolm and you had hotdogs again."

He half ran and half hobbled up the drive and over the steps with an unaccustomed pace. That only served to make her suspicious. And, in her suspicion, she called out to him through the window, "What are you up to now?" He didn't answer though she knew he heard her.

She drove to the cemetery with one eye on the road and one eye on Albert. She stopped checking him when he asked, "What?" But she was still wondering. Her wonder took a back seat to her concern when they arrived at the cemetery and found Tommy at his late wife's great aunt's grave. Neither was surprised to find him there.

"Your sampler is ready," she whispered, out of respect for the environs. "You can come by and get it wherever you like."

"Thank you," he whispered back.

After respects were paid and goodbyes were said, Albert suggested they have a little walk.

"Here?" She questioned. "Albert, my feet are aching. I have to get off of them."

"Just a little…" he said. Her took her hand and started leading her down the beaten grass between the rows of graves. "Adele, I've been thinking."

"Oh, no, that usually means trouble for somebody." She joked. Albert grinned and talked as they walked.

"Adele, children are inquisitive creatures. They ask questions. Answers need to be provided…besides; a body needs a proper resting place. You can't expect a man to get to heaven from the bottom of the sea." She didn't notice he stopped. He waved his arm in a motion intent to draw attention to where his hand lay. It was a marble gravestone. It bore a twin screw steamship cut into an oval background. The inscription below read:

Harry Andrew Wallace

1908-1928

Husband, Father, Man O'the Sea

He was a little nervous. He wondered if he had gone too far. But, it was too late to turn back now. "I bought three other plots. You'll be next to Harry, me next to you, and Isabelle next to me."

Her heart was overwhelmed. It seemed as if her lungs were not filling to their capacity. She took a deep breath and let it out slowly. She truly didn't know what to think. It was as if they were a real family. He loved her. She knew that was true. She looked at Harry's stone. The grief of the past and the comfort of the present and the fear of the future raced through her mind. What to say? How should she respond? Then, it struck her. She had learned from the master.

"Why Albert Pritchard, I thought you were an agnostic."

"Well," he explained. "He's been pretty good to me lately." Adele kissed her hand and placed it on Harry's name. Then, she turned to her adoptive father.

"I love it", she quietly stated. "And I love you, too. Let's go home."

As they walked back to the car, Adele slipped her hands into the crook of his arm. He knew that she was sincere in her claim. And his heart grew from that knowledge.

Chapter Twenty

A flickering lantern appeared across the bay and curious eyes wondered who might be walking the opposite shore on this night. The light grew and became a fire in the mind of the viewers. Perhaps driftwood was being collected and a bonfire started, signaling the start of an evening of revelry down by the water. Attention grew and conversation lessened. Soon the bonfire transformed into an orange arc rising above the tree line hidden previously by the dark of night. A slim ribbon of light was cast across the bay waters. Silence befell the viewers as they watched the moon rise and the ribbon widen into a pathway, inviting passage to those who can walk on water. Spellbound, all who witnessed this miracle sat in awe and whispered about the unusual orange hue of the moon tonight. As the earth, in perpetual rotation, moved the moon from view, the path disappeared and conversation on the porch that preceded its arrival continued.

Abner Thomas leaned against the center column of the porch taking in the magnificent show that nature had provided them. The chair he had previously occupied continue to rock slowly back and forth until the mechanical energy that propelled it weakened to the point that it could no longer move the wooden structure. "Now that was a sight to behold," he announced as he returned to his chair.

"Yes it was, my friend," said a rocking Albert. "That why I love this state. Everyday is a show and every scene is a picture that people in the cities pay good money to hang in their homes."

Adele was unusually quiet. She lost in thought; wondering if her Momma saw a pathway like that. Was such a sight the enticement she needed to convince her to cross over to the other shore? She wondered that if she took such a path, would it lead her to Harry. The life inside of her kicked her back to her senses. The answer to the first question she would never know. Touching her swollen abdomen answered the second. Nothing had to lead her to her beloved. He had been with her all the time.

The patient room of the Pritchard home underwent a major renovation. After the furniture was moved to the attic, Malcolm attacked the room with fervor, with Millie providing the supervision. The cherub wallpaper was stripped from the wall, the plaster repaired and the walls re-sized. The paint was stripped and sanded from the doors, windows and wood trim. The floors were sanded smooth to reduce any possibility of splinters finding their way into a tiny foot. Any inkling that death had ever visited the room had been painstakingly removed. Abner Thomas had delivered furniture Albert purchased in Portland; crib, dresser and rocking chair for mother.

When the work was done, a sparkling new nursery emerged. The room that had for years eased the dying out of the world was ready to welcome the living into it. The walls were ready for wallpaper, but the pattern had not been decided. Adele had purchased two patterns, toy wood trains pulling the letters of the alphabet for boys and rows of Raggedy Anns, each holding a letter of the alphabet in case a baby girl joined their family. Picture frames lay in the crib. On top of them were cross-stitched samplers expressing the joys of motherhood and the wonderment of youth. There were two sets of each; one with blue stitching, one with pink.

The decision was made on August the eighteenth in the year of our Lord nineteen hundred and twenty nine when Harry Albert Wallace was escorted head first from the womb of his anxious mother by the caring, gentle hands of his proud, self-proclaimed grandfather. The attending physician, guardian, and patriarch declared mother and child healthy. Both were bathed and tucked into bed by Millie, playing the role of midwife.

Albert retired to the den to greet the well-wishers who had overflowed into the sitting room and kitchen. A steady stream of women climbed up the stairs to *ooh* and *ahh* over the baby until Millie, in her new-found authority, sent them off to join their men folk so that mother and child could rest. Downstairs the men smoked fat cigars and, in a rare occasion for the Pritchard house, toasted the blessed event with a glass of Napoleon brandy, Jack Drucker providing the libations, Thomas Avery abstaining. Poor Malcolm Blake had but a few puffs of his cigar and one sip of brandy when Millie reached into the room and pulled him out by the collar. The house roared with laughter with the single men proclaiming, "Never me," and the married men rebuking them for their youthful, foolish beliefs.

Malcolm hung the toy train wallpaper and Millie framed and hung the blue samplers, despite objections of her hard-working husband.

"Damn woman, can't you wait until the paper dries?" Millie could not wait. When the nursery was complete and awaiting its new occupant, the volunteers entered the room across the hall to hug the mother and kiss the baby. They closed the door on their way out to ensure the tranquility of the room's occupants and headed downstairs. Millie went searching for the praise and accolades of a job well done, and Malcolm went in search of his brandy.

Adele lay in bed and listened to the sounds of joy and life that she knew must be coming out of every window in the house. She contrasted that to the sounds of despair and suffering she heard coming through the walls of the Bangor Home for the Feeble Minded. She was suddenly in awe of the balance of life and she felt in her heart that though evil and pain walked among us, goodness and healing are always on guard. Feeling safe in her home, she snuggled into her son and slept.

Chapter Twenty-one

The joy Adele felt on the day that little Harry was born remained and grew stronger as Harry did. He was a happy baby who developed into a delightful toddler who evolved into a wonderful child. Albert and Malcolm did everything they could to spoil him, but Adele and Millie's discipline kept him on an even keel, although Adele, at some times, had her doubts about Millie.

After years of tasting her own cooking, Millie had gained quite a bit of weight. So much that she took to wearing long, flowing dresses that came down to her ankles. Whenever Adele found scribbling on the walls or a toy truck on the stairs, she would call him using all three names. "Harry Albert Wallace!" This only proved to forewarn the boy who would make a mad dash to the kitchen and hide under Millie's dress. His mother would come looking for him, and Millie would never give him away. Seeing his little feet poking out from under Millie's hem, Adele would lose her anger and walk out of the room wondering aloud, "Now where do suppose that little imp has gotten off to?"

Despite the efforts of those who coddled him maybe a little too much, he was a delightful and engaging child. He would play for hours on the porch with his toy cars and was usually quiet when adults were talking. But sometimes he would forget his manners, as he did one day in August of 1939. It was days before his birthday and he felt the need to place some casual hints on his choice of presents. Adele was trying to talk to Albert about the decision that was made at last April's town meeting to hire a constable for the town. Feeling that the government that rules the least rules the best, Adele opposed the decision.

"I don't see why we need a constable. The sheriff's office has always done a fine job patrolling the roads. We're not in Bangor. Just how much crime goes on around here that we need a constable?"

Harry was pushing a toy truck across the planks on the porch making a clacking noise as the tires rolled from plank to plank.

"CHOO-CHOO, look Momma, I have a train."

"Bumper and I are talking, Harry." Albert was dubbed Bumper when Harry learned to talk. He loved the mispronunciation so much than he began to insist that everyone call him by that name.

"Yes, Momma," Harry said dutifully.

"You know you're right," Bumper chimed in. "It does sort of sounds like a train. But remember the one we saw in the Sears & Roebuck Catalog, the electric one with the track and the little station? Now that's a train."

"Yeah, Bumper, that's a train!" Adele looked over at Harry's accomplice and smiled.

"Could you help me roll some yarn?" Adele had taken up crocheting Afghans. She had permeated the town with samplers and decided it was time to move on. Besides, Afghans were functional and she had come to a point in her life that function was more important than form. Albert was not too pleased. As much as he grew to hate the cross-stitching, he hated the afghans even more. He would complain, "The damn things get stuck in your toes." And to make matters worse, she would have him hold the skein of yarn between his hands while she carefully rolled it into useable balls. "Can't you find a hobby that I don't have to participate in?"

He helped Adele roll the skeins into balls. This time there were only two, one white and one a light blue. He rubbed the feeling back into his hands and, now out of habit, into his leg and opened the *Grapes of Wrath*. Before he began to read, he gave his grandson a reassuring nod. The train was in the bag.

A gaggle of geese flew in off the coast and headed right for the house. They spied the humans sitting there and rolled south, squawking in unison as they passed. The whole episode startled Harry and he leaped into his Bumper's waiting arms.

"They're just Canada geese," Momma said calmly as she started her first row of the afghan. Harry released Bumper and was a little embarrassed about his fear.

"Well, they scared the bejeezus out of me!"

"Harry Albert Wallace," his mother scolded.

"But, Bumper says it!" Adele looked at Albert over her newly prescribed eyeglasses. Always knowing when it was best to change the subject, Bumper pointed to the geese as they rounded the yard and made their way back to the bay.

"Harry," he said, "You see how they fly in a V shape?"

"Yes, Bumper, I see the V." Adele didn't look. She had heard it before.

"You notice how one leg of the V looks longer than the other one," he continued his grandson's education.

"Yes, Bumper." His attention was growing.

"You know why that is?"

Here it comes, Adele thought and smiled.

"No, Bumper."

"Because there are more geese on that side." He slapped his leg and broke out in laughter. Harry looked at Bumper, then, puzzled, at his mother. She glanced at him with a welcome to my world look, and shrugged her shoulders.

Suddenly Albert stopped laughing and jerked back into his rocker. Then, he lunged forward and jerked back again.

"Albert!" Adele screamed and jumped up and sprawled her yarn all over the porch.

"Bumper!" Harry cried in terrifying shock.

Albert attempted to rise and fell back into his rocker. A coagulated lump of blood that had formed in his femoral artery tore loose and traveled through the blood passage until it reached the pump. His aorta, with an inner diameter that had diminished over the years, denied the clot passage. The resulting dam stopped the flow of blood to his atrium. The ventricle flexed violently seeking the blood it was supposed to deliver throughout the aging body. The jerking Adele and Harry witnessed was his body's battle to circulate its blood. His rise and fall was the surrender.

At that moment, on the porch of the white two-story colonial where Dr. Albert Pritchard healed and hurt, loved and hated, and laughed and cried, he passed from this earth.

Chapter Twenty-two

Albert was taken to Jenkins and Smith to lie in wait. The white two story perched on the banks of the Penobscot was flooded with people offering condolences. They bestowed the grieving with flowers and food as they flowed in and out of the house. The dining room and kitchen table were covered with baked goods. The refrigerator that Albert bought to replace the icebox (which, at first, Adele did not trust) was crammed with casseroles. The den took on the appearance of a greenhouse.

Adele was dressed in black, and Harry was clothed in fear and sadness. He had slept in his mother's bed for the past two nights. Adele had to go to his room twice on the night his Bumper died, after hearing him crying from the dreams that woke him. She was determined to put him in his own bed on this night. She felt that after the initial shock, he had to face his fears.

Sheriff Poulin (who tried unsuccessfully to fill the shoes of the retired Sheriff Farnham) had sent out a deputy to take his report. All there was left to do was bury Albert. At first she thought she would have him buried in his lab coat, tongue depressor and reflex hammer in his breast pocket and stethoscope around his neck. She decided against that idea, realizing that there was much more to the man than his just profession. She chose a three-piece gray herringbone suit. He loved it. She always hated it. Her first choice for a tie was one that Harry had picked out to give him for Christmas. It was ugly as sin, but he wore it out of the house and changed it in the car. She settled for one she had purchased. It was off white with men on horseback with dogs at the heel. She had bought it for his birthday because it reminded her of the parlor, and the years she spent under his tutelage as she learned the art of healing. She held it softly against her cheek. Then she folded Harry's tie and slipped into his suit jacket pocket, just in case it was permissible for one to change their tie on the other side. If it was, she knew he would have it on when she joined him in heaven. She ironed the white shirt with a faded mustard stain that he took to wearing on his trips to Bangor. Finally, she shined his shoes until she could see her reflection in them. She wiped the tears that fell on them and loaded his burial attire into the car.

She called to Harry who was sitting down at the shore. She was going to drop him off to stay with Tommy at the lumberyard. When she called to ask him, Tommy responded, "Are you kidding? I love that boy." Tommy's own sons were gone and had seemed to forget that he ever existed.

"Tommy," Adele told him. "Take your sampler down." He was putting it in a drawer of his desk as she spoke.

When Adele arrived at Jenkins and Smith, she saw the Reverend McIntosh's car parked out in front of it. She made sure to leave enough room for him to get out when he left before she left. Adele took no stock in the Reverend.

Few people knew the secret of Adele's marriage. Sheriff Farnham contracted cancer and died an agonizing death. Adele was with him in his final days and watched his body rot away. Though she was no longer a nurse, she was still a friend. On the day he died she had cleaned the waste he left in his bed and on his body and was trying to feed him some chicken broth. He reached and took the hand holding the spoon and, with a weak voice and fading eyes, he spoke two words that gave meaning to her life. "You care."

She had buried Miss Jonas and was making preparations to bury Albert. The town clerk had lost her husband in a hunting accident and had met and married a circus clown. They had long since moved to Sarasota, Florida. Tommy she trusted with her life. And that left only the good Reverend. She used to fear him, but had since come to learn that he was a cowardly man. To inform on her would be to implicate him and he lacked the fortitude to do that.

When she entered the office he was trying to negotiate his fee.

"Reverend, have you been asked to preside?" Mr. Jenkins questioned.

"Who else would officiate in a service in my church?" Reverend McIntosh was a tall, thin man with skin so smooth one would think he stole it from a woman. He lost his hair at an early age and covered it with a British driving cap that he thought made him look distinguished. He wore button-collared shirts that his mother kept washed and ironed. It was rumored by the ladies of the church that should he find the smallest wrinkle in them, he would deposit them in the clothes hamper for her to wash and iron again. It the cold months he wore a black wool overcoat and traded it for a cashmere sweater in the spring. The mere sight of the man disturbed Adele.

Adele entered the room unnoticed. "If you're discussing Dr. Pritchard, I can assure you that you will not be presiding over the service, church be damned."

"Madam?" His tone was indigent. "I *am* the spiritual leader of this fine community!"

"You are an ass. You profess to be a man of the cloth, but the only time you open a Bible is when you think someone will lay some money into it. You show up on Sunday morning to condemn folks for doing the same things you do all week, and then, you disappear until the next Sunday, save for buzzing about town in that little roadster you worship. You neither comfort the sick nor tend to the poor. I do not care for you and Dr. Pritchard cared for you even less. I will not besmirch his honor to have you standing over his grave waiting for him to hold up an envelope between his fingers!"

The Reverend arose stiff backed from his chair. "I can assure you, Madam, that your blasphemy will not go unnoticed by my congregation." With that he stormed out of the room. Mr. Jenkins looked at the clothes Adele was holding.

"Oh, good, Mrs. Wallace," he said, "You've brought his suit." He examined them briefly. "Yes, an excellent choice. Excellent."

That night after Adele put Harry to bed, in his bed, she went into the den to write Albert's eulogy. She wrote a few sentences, wadded up the paper, and threw it in the wastebasket. She repeated this process until she found the

172

right words. It was one o'clock in the morning and the wastebasket was overflowing. She read it one more time and told herself that Albert would be pleased. Even Isabelle would be pleased.

"Oh my God", she whispered. "Isabelle!"

Chapter Twenty-three

Harry was hungry in the morning. He ate three eggs, four pieces of bacon, and three pieces of toast with grape jelly.

"Child," Millie warned, "If you don't slow down, you're gonna get as big as me." This only encouraged him to eat more. He thought it would be keen to be as big as Millie. She could knock Malcolm against the wall with a swing of her hips. And even at the age of ten, her lap was still as comfortable to him as the big boy bed that Bumper bought when he grew too tall for his crib. Adele entered the kitchen just as he drank a large gulp of his orange juice.

"Hurry and finish, honey", Adele told him. "You're going to visit Uncle Tommy today." Harry started to wipe the orange juice pulp off of his lip with the sleeve of his shirt. Adele cleared her throat and he stopped in mid-swipe and picked up his napkin.

"Sorry, Momma", he offered. "Sometimes I forget my manners."

"…As did your father." She used her hand to muss up his hair. "That's why I'm here."

On the way to Bangor Adele dropped Harry off at the lumberyard. Tommy saw them pull up and stowed his bulldog sampler in the drawer. That night he would take it home and hang it in his bedroom in hopeful anticipation that Harry's visits would become a regular routine. Adele was upset and they walked and talked as Harry drew pictures of trucks on the ledger of Tommy's desk.

"I'm scared Tommy," Adele said as they passed an endless stacks of sawn boards.

"You've never been scared a day in your life. You're the bravest person I know."

"Well, I'm scared now. I don't know if I can go through with it."

Tommy decided to come to the aid of his savior. "We'll drop Harry off at the Blake's, and I'll go with you."

"No dear," Adele said, patting his hand. "This is my cross to bear." Adele didn't know what she was going to say when she got to Bangor, or even if her plan was workable. But she intended to have Isabelle seated next to her on the return trip, if only for the funeral, but hopefully forever.

The Bangor Home for the Feeble Minded, now called the Maine State Mental Health Hospital, seemed a little nicer than the last time she pulled up its drive. People in blue colored pajamas were walking around outside amidst smiling attendants in starched white uniforms. Flowers were growing in the gardens and a group of laughing blue wearers and one happy white wearer were enjoying a picnic at a table, being served by a group of ladies in street clothes. Adele didn't notice as much screaming and howling as she did on her first trip. Maybe things had changed, or maybe she had. Perhaps, she reasoned, it was the weather. It was the dead of winter when she first saw these grounds. After the initial awestricken wonder of winter's white blanket, people often draw inside in the cold months, and sadness and depression leak out. Whatever the cause, she noted a change and was optimistic.

Dr. Livingston was as Albert had described him, albeit older. He was sitting back in his chair with the ankle of one leg resting on the knee of the other. As she relayed her story and told her intentions, he continuously tapped a fountain pen on the arm of his chair. (Albert had told her about his annoying pipe habits. She assumed that the doctor had stopped smoking, and had replaced one pacifier with another.) He occasionally stopped tapping long enough to lean forward, removed the pen's cap, and write something in a folder in front of him. Replacing the cap, he continued to tap. His head bobbed up and down excessively until she wanted to take a hold of it with both hands and still its motion. When she got to the part of taking Isabelle home, the bobbing stopped on its own.

"Am I to take it, Mrs. Wallace is it?" She offered no response. She saw him write her name down during a cession of tapping. "Am I to take it," he repeated, "that you have taken over the affairs of the late Dr. Pritchard?"

"You may."

"Well, you must know there are expenses associated with the services we render here; nominal to be sure. We are under the blanket of the Bureau of Mental Health, but our budget is trifling considering the work we do. Dr. Pritchard was very generous with his contributions, unlike some relations who would just as soon let their loved ones rot...." Adele had heard enough.

176

"You shall be paid."

"Harrumph. Well then, I'm not too sure I can condone your decision, but I'll leave it in your hands. However, before making such a rash pronouncement, you may want to take the time to meet with Mrs. Pritchard. If you would kindly go down the hall and into the second room on the left, she will meet you there." Her dislike for the man grew deeper.

The room he directed her to was small, no more than ten feet by ten feet. Its walls were at one time painted white, but had yellowed over the years. The bare light bulb that hung high in the ceiling cast a shadow behind the room's only furnishing, two straight-backed wooden chairs. The room was more fitting for interrogation than for visiting. Adele brushed the dust out of one of the chairs with her hand and sat in it. She was about to get up and brush the dust from the other when the door opened.

Two men in uniforms that had not ever seen an iron entered. The buttons that ran up the sides of their smocks were fastened only to the shoulder, and revealed dingy white undershirts beneath. One was smoking a cigarette. The woman who slumped between them was not Mrs. Pritchard, not the Mrs. Pritchard who tormented Adele in her teens. It was not even the Mrs. Pritchard that slapped her face on the upstairs landing on the last day she slept in the Pritchard home. She wore a thick cotton waistcoat whose cuffs had been sewed closed and secured with a leather strap on one and a brass buckle on the other. Her arms were crossed and pulled around her waist; the buckle fastened, imprisoning her in her attire. Under the coat, she wore a plain cotton dress devoid of color. Her hair was so matted that a comb would have been unless; shears would be it's only redemption. She smelled of the sardine factory. The attendants sat her, not too gently, in the chair. "We'll be right outside the door," advised one of the men.

Adele pointed to the straitjacket. "Is that thing necessary?"

"Oh, yes ma'am," answered the smoker, "It's very necessary."

When they exited and closed the door, Adele pulled her chair in front of the woman who used to be Isabelle Pritchard. Isabelle was rocking back and forth and tugging at her restraints in a vain attempt to free herself.

"Mrs. Pritchard?" Adele was shaken. She closed her eyes to calm herself. When she opened them again, she repeated the first words she had spoken to Isabelle in twelve years. This time it was a statement, not a question. "Mrs. Pritchard." The woman didn't know Adele was in the room. "It's me, Adele Walla…Adele Abbott. Do you hear me Mrs. Pritchard?" Her only response was to rock and tug. Adele put her hand on the knee of the cotton dress. "Mrs. Pritchard, Dr Pritchard has passed away."

The widow Pritchard looked up at Adele. "DO YOU HAVE ANY GUM?"

"Did you hear me, Mrs. Pritchard? Albert is dead."

"..GUM, I WANT GUM!"

Adele was horrified. "Isabelle!"

"IT'S A BELL! GONG! IT"S A BELL! GONG!"

The door flew opened. The frightened patient quieted and leaned back in her chair and froze. "It's okay," Adele told the men and the door closed. When she looked up she was greeted by a devilish stare that turned into an evil grin. Isabelle's rounded her mouth. She opened and closed it, mimicking a fish. "You're a fishwife," she said in a low growl. "A fishwife whore. FISH WIFE WHORE, FISH WIFE WHORE!" She lunged at Adele toppling both of them and the chairs to the floor. The deranged woman jumped to her feet and started, hectically, running around the room. FISH WIFE WHORE, FISH WHORE! IT'S A BELL, GONG; IT'S A BELL, GONG!" The attendants rushed into the room and tackled her to the floor. They wrestled control of her and dragged her screaming from the room. One gripped the shoulder of the jacket; the other had her by the hair of her head. As they left Adele, still sitting on the floor, noticed that Mrs. Dr. Albert Pritchard wore no panties. Adele got up off the floor and straightened herself. Leaving the chairs where they lay, she went out, closing the door behind her. Dr. Livingston was standing with his ankles crossed, leaning against the frame of the doorway of his office. "It's a shame," he said. "Pritchard was a nice fellow; misguided, but a likeable chap, nonetheless." She started over towards him with the intentions of slapping his face. He eyes grew larger and he stepped back inside his office and closed the door. Adele heard a key turn in the lock. She left the building and then the grounds. She cried until she reached Jonasport Hill.

Before collecting Harry, Adele paid a visit to the Thomas'. Mrs. Thomas was delighted to see her and made her chamomile tea. When Abner returned from an errand, he was equally delighted. "Adele has a favor to ask of you, Abner," Mrs. Thomas said coyly. Albert's chess partner turned to Adele.

"Of course, dear, anything you need."

"You had better hear me out first. I don't want that preacher anywhere near Albert's funeral. And Mrs. Thomas agrees with me."

Mrs. Thomas nodded her head. "That's right," she said. "Doc Pritchard just might rise up and chase him off the grounds."

Adele smiled and continued. "I think, and Mrs. Thomas agrees with me, that you should preside over the services. He always considered you his closest friend."

"That's how I felt about him. But, dear, I ain't been in a church in a month of Sundays. Mrs. Thomas can attest to that."

"Amen," his wife said piously. Abner stuck his tongue out at her and turned to Adele.

"But dear, I wouldn't know what to say. I wouldn't know where to begin."

Adele retrieved the eulogy from her handbag and held it out to him.

"Just read this and whatever else comes from your heart."

"But, Adele…."

"He'd be honored," Mrs. Thomas said, ending the debate. Adele was still holding out the sheet of paper. Abner took it from her as carefully as someone would take a bomb. "Its not going bite you, Abner", his wife promised.

"Yeah, well, I just might bite you", he replied. He stayed up longer that night memorizing it than Adele had spent in writing it.

Supper was on the stove when Harry and Adele arrived home. Adele found a note between her silverware and her plate.

Malcolm called me. He says he is feeling poorly. So, I went to tend to him. Would you mind doing the dishes? I could do them tomorrow, but I am afraid of drawing ants.

Love,

Millie

P S That awful psykiatrust called and wants you to call him.

Adele fixed Harry a plate and went into the den to call Livingston. She had no idea why he would be trying to contact her, but was relatively sure that it had something to do with money. After talking to him, she dearly wished that she was right. Dr. Livingston regretted to inform her that Isabelle had escaped from her escorts. In an attempt to elude capture she ran into the stairwell on the fourth floor. She was still in her straitjacket and was unable to grab on to the railing and unfortunately plunged over it. The fall broke her neck. It was regrettable. *He regrets that he can no longer extort money from Albert*, she thought when gave her the news. Whatever they discussed in the visitation room must have disturbed her terribly. She had been doing so well. Anyway, that was water under the bridge and he needed to know how Adele wanted the corpse disposed of.

Adele buried Dr. Pritchard and his wife at the same service. There was a turnout that exceeded the burial of Miss Jonas. Tommy was a great comfort to Adele and Harry. Abner did a wonderful job on the eulogy. He never once looked at the sheet of paper he clutched in his hands. The words he added spoke of a noble life and when he reached the part of *beloved friend*, his wife cried. No words were spoken over Isabelle.

Adele did purchase a tombstone for her grave. Albert had already morbidly bought his. All that was left for the stone-cutter to do was chisel in the date of his death. Adele thought long and hard on what to say on

Isabelle's. In the end she chose the only words she could think of to sum up the life of the woman.

Isabelle Pritchard

Doctor's Wife

Chapter Twenty-four

With the Pritchards secure in their final resting place, Adele tried to get Harry back into a normal routine. She noticed he had resumed his habit of going down to the water where he would sit staring off at the other shore. It used to be a thrill of his that made her uneasy. Now it seemed to put her at ease. Before too long, mother and son got on with their life.

A letter arrived addressed to Adele Wallace from the law firm of Oakhurst and Smiley. It advised her that she was named in the will of Albert Pritchard, M.D. Could she please contact their office to arrange for the reading of the will? Adele scheduled and attended the meeting. Albert had instructed that his dairy and egg farms be sold and the proceeds put into escrow to provide for the care of his wife, Isabelle Gong Pritchard, currently a patient at the Bangor Home for the Feeble Minded. In the event of her demise, the remainder of the monies would be put into a trust to finance research into the causes and possible treatment of mental illness. It was stipulated that no monies would be invested until such time as Dr. Charles Livingston, staff psychiatrist, was no longer affiliated with that or any other medical or government institution in the state of Maine. The remainder of his estate, including the home in Jonasport, Maine and the acreage in Scotia County currently leased to the Epstein Potato Company was to be awarded to Adele Susannah Wallace, also known as Adele Susannah Abbott.

Malcolm had begun to feel poorly more often than not. Millie begged Adele to examine him. But, as it had been so long since she had practiced nursing, and with the advent of new medicines and medical discoveries, Adele convinced him to take his doctor's advice and admit himself into the hospital. After a series of tests and examinations it was determined that he suffered from diabetes. He was sent home with a new diet and a favorable prognosis. He was to adopt a less strenuous lifestyle, and Millie, regrettably, resigned from her position to stay home and keep an eye on him. She entrusted Adele with her fear that Malcom's sweet tooth would be the death of him should she not be there to guide him. The truth was she felt that her place was by the side of her sick husband. Despite the doctor's optimism, Millie suspected that he could be taken from her and wanted to spend all the time with him she could, lest her fears proved to be true. They lived a quiet and happy life on the money they had saved from the years of employment they enjoyed in the white two-story colonial. Adele had learned a few things from the time she spent nosing around in Millie's kitchen, so

Harry and she were not likely to starve. And whenever something needed fixing or lifting, Tommy was over before she could hang up the telephone.

Tommy had become a regular fixture at Adele's house. When Harry started schoolyard baseball, Tommy was right next to Adele in the bleachers at every game. When Adele starred in the church's yearly performance of the *Peabody Pew*, Tommy was on the front row. This year proceeds were to go to purchase a shingles for the chapel and Tommy had volunteered to help install it. The Reverend McIntosh, however, was conspicuously absent for the play, having taking an unannounced sabbatical to Cape Cod.

There was talk about town that Adele and Tommy might get together. Adele quashed those rumors during a meeting of the Woman's Auxiliary.

"Do you think you and Tommy will ever tie the knot?" The question came from one of the younger members.

"Tie the knot?" Adele questioned.

"You know, marry."

"No dear, there's only been one man in my life. And he's resting on the bottom of the ocean."

"Ah-h-h-h," sang the chorus of ladies in romantic jubilation.

"But don't you ever miss…well…you know… it?" the younger lady dared to ask her, although she blushed from the asking. Adele was busily inspecting a jar of green beans to ensure the seal was intact. They were preparing a shipment of food to a Maine town that had a disastrous year. It would not do to add botulism to the list of tragedies that had befallen the residents of Bar Harbor. The fire that had started on October the 17th, a disaster that would forever be remembered as the Great Fire, destroyed over 170 homes in the Mount Desert Island region of Maine. And, although it was over two hours to the area where the wealthy played in the summer, the residents were still neighbors, and the Woman's Auxiliary of Jonasport was in the business of helping neighbors. She put the approved jar into a wood crate.

"If you are referring to sexual intercourse, I'm afraid I'll have to insist that is not a subject of conversation for ladies." Adele could sense the disappointment in the room. She glanced around and saw most of the members were pretending to be inspecting their jars. A few of the bolder ones had their eyes trained on her. "All right, you Nosy Nates, I'll tell you." All inspection stopped and all eyes turned to Adele. "Once I took little Harry to New York City. We went by train and stayed in a tall hotel. We visited the Statue of Liberty and took the elevator all the way to the top. We looked out over the water, right through the lady's crown. It was very exciting. It was the thrill of a lifetime." The anticipation in the room was growing. No one knew where this was going, but all assumed it was going to be juicy. Adele picked up a can of pickled beets and inspected its seal. "But I did it once, and see no reason to go through all the trouble necessary to do it again."

"Oh-h-h," sang the chorus.

Adele was sitting on the porch on a brisk September evening peeling an orange with her momma's bone-handled paring knife. She was wrapped in an afghan with a silk scarf tied around her head to prevent the wind off the water from destroying her hairdo. Tommy was helping Harry enjoy his new Schwinn bicycle, which he had gotten him for his twelfth birthday. Harry was on his new bicycle and Tommy was on his old bike. They were on the starting line of their tenth race of the evening.

Two weeks before the big day, Harry and Tommy had been in Harry's bedroom practicing arithmetic. But unlike many other bedrooms in many other towns, in the Wallace home in the town of Jonasport, the child was the teacher and the adult was the pupil. Tommy, having neglected his studies as a child, had now begun to realize the necessity of arithmetic in his job at the lumberyard. The teacher was posing a question that he had prepared prior to tonight's lesson. The Sears & Roebuck Catalog was opened on Harry's desk.

"Now Tommy," the teacher began. "I have already counted the toys on these six pages." He quickly flipped the six pages and returned to the first page. "I can tell you that each page has the same number of toys. Count the toys on the first page and tell me how many toys are on the six." As Tommy began to count the toys, he noticed that an advertisement for a Schwinn bicycle had been circled. The caption that read, 'your boy will love it' was underlined. Tommy continued to count, and then taking pencil and paper proceeded to the calculation stage of the problem. After a bit of erasing and some finger counting that Harry put a stop to ("In your head," he said), Tommy proudly announced the answer.

"One hundred and forty-four", Tommy proudly announced.

"Good," teacher stated. "You get a star."

Tommy parked the old bicycle and came up over to the steps and flopped down in a rocker, leaving Harry to zoom around on his own.

"Oh," he protested. "That boy is gonna wear me out."

"You spoil him," Adele accused, dividing her orange into sections.

Tommy pondered a thought that often prevented sleep from coming to him at night.

"Maybe if I spoiled my own a little more, they'd still be with me." Harry was not that much older than his stepsons when their mother dragged them up from the sardine factory at the close of the season. At the time, he had little use for them. After the death of their mother, Miss Jonas, and then Adele, instilled a desire in him to be a better father. No more than a month after he finished his new home, their natural father, a merchant sailor and opium addict, came to town and reentered their life. As soon as they were of age, they followed their natural father in his trade and, Tommy feared, his addiction. He never saw or heard from them again.

"You can't change the past, Thomas." She called him Thomas when she was serious, and when she was about to chastise him. "You can only alter the future." She handed him a slice of orange. He popped it into his mouth and made a vow to himself that he did not realized came out aloud.

"...and alter it, I will."

Chapter Twenty-five

Adele abhorred the use of alcohol. She blamed the vice for the laziness of her father, the perversion of Tibias Anderson, and the suicide of her mother. So it filled her with pride and admiration to see how Tommy Avery shook off the grip it had taken on him in his early life. Sometimes as she drove by the center-chimney cape that he erected when his sons were still with him, she would stop and admire it, shaking her head in wonder and grinning like the Cheshire cat. He had bulldozed the sty that his wife died in and he and the boys had moved in with Miss Jonas until he built his new home. He had intended for Miss Jonas to move in with them, though she laughed at the idea when he presented it. She died in the winter before the roof was on. And, when she died, the town took possession of her home for back taxes. Being a direct descendent of the town's father carried a lot of weight in life, but in death one is just a delinquent taxpayer and the devil will get his due. Tommy and the boys had to move into the unfinished house. Tommy worked on it evenings and nights (and even on Sundays) in the dead of winter until it was complete. And throughout the hardships he had to endure, he never once returned to the bottle.

When Tommy announced that he was buying Drucker's Lumber, Adele was not surprised. The money he had saved by not drinking had accumulated in the bank. With a sizable down payment at his disposal, the bank loaned him enough to make the purchase. Jack Drucker bragged about town that, though he was retiring, Drucker's Lumber would always be a fixture in Jonasport. He was sure that Avery would not change the name of the company. He had the good sense to understand that, in Soctomah County, the name Drucker meant quality and Avery would be foolish to change it. Besides, he reckoned that after giving him such a break in life, Tommy would be obliged to keep the name out of respect, so great was his and the other employees devotion to him. The ink wasn't dry on the deed before Tommy had the sign removed and replaced with a smaller one that read *Avery & Sons Lumberyard*. He was forever hopeful.

When Harry turned fifteen, he got his first job at Avery and Sons. Tommy had taught him to drive and he wanted to buy a car. Adele had attempted to teach him, but the boy terrified her behind the wheel, so she enlisted Tommy's help.

Harry bought his car the next year. It was a 1941 Ford Super Deluxe Convertible. Adele personally saw nothing super about the old junk heap. The seats were torn, the top was worn to the thickness of a bed sheet, and it was half black, half rust. It leaked oil that stained the driveway, and the spare tire was so bald that his mother claimed she could see the air in it. But Harry loved it.

Adele offered to help him buy a new car, but he wouldn't have it. And she was proud of him for feeling that way. (However, four years later, when she bought him a brand new 1948 Chrysler Royal Coupe for his high school graduation present, he did not complain. While shopping for it the dealer tried to sell her on the car by telling her it sported a 251-cubic-inch straight Flathead engine, the "spitfire 6." That meant nothing to her, but the idea that Chrysler had installed an automatic transmission that year made her feel Harry would be safer in it. Having no clutch to burn out might put a stop to the rapid takeoffs he enjoyed in his old Ford).

Adele had come to recognize the sound of Harry's rust bucket, as she was fond of calling it. When it came down the road she could tell from the deceleration or acceleration whether he would come home after work or would make the turn around horny corner (a name she had grown sick of hearing) to head up to Tommy's house. More often than not it was acceleration. Some mothers might be hurt by the fact that their son would want to be somewhere other than home. But Adele knew that a boy needed a father, and Tommy was the closet thing Harry had to one. And as soon as he could free his hand off the wheel without rolling over into bay, he would always honk a greeting on that sick-sounding horn. Thus she felt satisfied that he had acknowledged her existence.

But with graduation quickly approaching Adele secretly wished he would decelerate and turn left a little more often than he did. Harry inherited his mother's intelligence and his Bumper's love of books. He was valedictorian of his class and had a number of acceptances to different colleges. Oh, he could be a royal pain. He ate like a horse and had no concept of how to scrape a dish and put it in the sink. He left his clothes wherever he might take them off. She repeatedly questioned how a boy who could dismantle a carburetor and put it back together with ease could not manage to put a roll of toilet paper in its carrier. He played that cursed radio into the wee hours of the morning. With his room right across from hers, she would have to get up and stuff an afghan under her door in order to get some sleep. But, all and all, she would just like to have him around a little bit longer.

She was dusting the bookcases and pondering these thoughts when she heard his car pull up. She had the urge to run out and see him, but she refrained. He came into the house and slammed the door, took off through the dining room, and ran up the stairs. She heard his door slam and apparently it failed to close, because she heard it slam again. She went up to him, but always respectful of his privacy, she knocked on the door.

"Come in, Ma." *Whatever happened to Momma?* He was sitting on his bed repeatedly slapping a baseball into his mitt. Adele sat next to him and the thought came to her how much he resembled his father.

"Tommy is moving, ma." He told her the whole story. She comforted him the best she could and reminded him of his evening commitment.

"Oh, crap," he said looking at his wristwatch.

"Harry!"

"Sorry ma." He changed his shirt, dropping the dirty one on the floor and raced off to pick up his sweetheart to go to the picture show. Adele picked up his shirt off the floor and put it into the laundry hamper. Then she went downstairs and sat in her Queen Anne chair to wait for Tommy.

She didn't have a long wait. Tommy didn't knock on the door. Accustomed as he had become to Adele's house, he just walked in. He went through the dining room and stopped in the foyer. Looking up the stairs he said, "Remember how proud you were to find those stair rods?" He was trying hard not to get to the point.

"I remember, Tommy. Come in and sit down."

Tommy obeyed and took a seat on the sofa. As he sat, Adele looked over at him.

"When were you going to tell me?"

"I've tried a hundred times before, Adele. I just couldn't find the words."

"But you found the words to tell Harry?"

Tommy jumped up and started pacing in the sitting room.

"He heard about it at the yard. He came over to my house just tonight and confronted me. What was I suppose to do? Lie to him?"

"No, Tommy. Sit down, please. You're making me dizzy."

Tommy sat down and started to explain his position. "There's a mill in Farmingdale and one in Worcester. Both are in receivership, but it's only from bad management. The market is there. I can turn them around. But I can't do it from Jonasport." He went on to explain the intricacies of the lumber business. How profit is gained and how profit is lost. He went on about the latest markets and new time saving machinery. He continued to talk until Adele thought her head would explode. She stopped him with a slight touch of her hand.

"I'm not upset that you're leaving, Tommy. I hate to see you go. And, of course, so will Harry. But, he'll be leaving soon, off to his own world, following his dreams. Life, Thomas Avery, is an ever-changing process. I am upset because you didn't tell me. Friends don't keep secrets from each other. Friends whisper secrets *to* each other. Is that not right?"

"It is."

"No more secrets?"

"No more secrets."

"Do you promise?"

"I promise." Adele stared into the cold fireplace, closed her eyes, and asked the dreaded question.

"When do you leave?"

"After Harry's graduation; I wanna see that boy get that diploma." Adele remembered something she told Dr. Pritchard on that subject years ago. *Graduation is for the parents.* "Well, I need to get going, Adele. I've got a lot to do."

"Tommy," Adele asked him, "When did you get so smart?"

Tommy looked down, swallowed, started to speak, and swallowed again. Finally, he looked her in the eye and announced, "When I decided to listen to you."

Chapter Twenty-six

Tommy did see Harry pick up his diploma. Afterward they had a graduation party at the house. Tommy excused himself and returned a short time later with Harry's new car. It had been hidden in the Blake's barn. Adele and Tommy sat on the porch as Harry zoomed away to pick up his sweetheart and friends. They roared back and forth past the house, honking a different, yet still sick sounding horn. After the new wore off, he returned his sweetheart and friends to their separate homes. Grins abounded when he pulled up in the driveway. He got out and cleaned his fingerprints off the door with his handkerchief. He walked up to the porch and leaned against the top railing. Adele remembered when he could only reach the lower rail and peek-a-boo through it.

"So Tommy, you need some help packing?"

Tommy could only nod that he did. He came off the porch and Harry threw an arm around his shoulder and the two friends walked to Harry's new car and drove away. When they left, Adele cried on the porch.

After the packing was done, Tommy gave the movers the destination address. He followed Harry back to the two-storied white colonial to bid goodbye to his oldest and dearest friend. Adele was sick of saying goodbye to people she loved, but persevered for the sake of Harry and Tommy. They had coffee and rocked on the porch, taking in the beauty of the bay that lay before them. Neither spoke. Sometimes the wonders of God's world took away the need to talk. As he got ready to go, Adele slipped back into the house and returned with a package. She handed it to Tommy and said, "Lest you forget." It was the picture his late wife had given him to deliver to Adele. Tommy remembered it well. Before he could comment Adele rushed back into the house. Harry tried to excuse his mother's emotional reaction, but Tommy stopped him.

"Take care of your mother, son."

"I will, Tommy." Tommy got into his car and started it up. As he put in reverse, he looked over at Harry and said, "I love you." He backed out of the driveway and pulled away. He was out of sight when Harry said, "I love you, too."

Harry moped around the house for the next few weeks. Being the ever-vigilant mother, Adele kept her eye on him. She was hanging sheets out to dry and spied him down by the bay, skipping stones across the water. She crossed the field and went down the steps to the shore. Without speaking she smoothed the back of her dress, took hold of the sides and sat on the last step. Harry did not turn around to greet his mother. He skipped another stone and asked, "Is Tommy my father?"

Adele had been a mother for eighteen years. No question could take her by surprise. "No, he isn't. I'm sure he'd like to be. Harry, you know your father died in a shipwreck. What makes you ask such a question?"

Harry turned around and confronted his mother. "I couldn't sleep last night, so I slipped out and went for a ride."

"I know you did."

"Well, I stopped at Clancy's...."

"...Harry, the roadhouse?"

"Ma, I'm of age. Besides I was just shooting billiards with some of the fellows. Ma, I remember Bumper telling Mr. Thomas that a bottle of liquor will sit on a shelf forever and never hurt a soul. It's the man, not the bottle."

Adele looked towards heaven. "Harry Albert Wallace, of all the things your grandfather said in the ten short years you knew him, that's the one thing you remember?" Harry came over and scooted her butt over with his and sat down.

"I remember that stupid geese joke." She smiled. "Ma, you know that guy that used to be a preacher? He was the guy that stole the money for the new roof."

"...McIntosh." She spat out the name. She remembered.

"Yeah, well he was there. And he's all liquored up and tells these women that he was sitting with, 'I married that kid's parents.' So, I didn't say anything. And he says, 'Did your dear father leave you the deed to the lumberyard before he skipped out?' I tell him that Tommy was not my father. And he says, 'Well, all I know is that I married the man who now owns Drucker's to your high and mighty mother.' So I get mad and smash him in the face and came home." He waited for either a denial or a lecture. He would accept either.

"Did you break his nose?" Harry jerked his head towards her and raised his eyebrows. Adele smoothed his brow with her fingers, and kissed his forehead. With the same stark honesty that she told Albert the story of little Harry's conception, she told Harry about his father. And as it had become her way, she made no omissions and waited for Harry to form his opinion. Harry embraced his mother with a newfound respect, not more than fifty feet away from the spot that his grandmother walked into the bay. They walked back up to the house together. On the way up Adele said, "Your Bumper would love to have seen that."

Chapter Twenty-seven

In the fall Harry enrolled in the Maine State College just north of Bangor. His scholarship included housing accommodations, but he declined them. He preferred to commute so that he might spend more time with his mother. It was a different life for both of them. But the love they shared made the adjustment easier. Soon, they adapted to their new routine. Harry spent a great deal of his time at home studying and Adele spent a great deal of her time, when he was not at home, worrying.

One evening an obscure, blind foreboding leaped from her head and landed on the small of her back. In an apparent attempt to return to its place of origin, it crawled up her spine, causing her to shiver in an effort to shake it off. She looked at the clock on the wall in the kitchen. Not contented with its accuracy, she went into the sitting room and checked the clock on the mantel. Satisfied that it was not time for Harry to return from school, she went back into the kitchen and looked out the window trying to discern the reason behind her anxiety. The fog was so thick she could not see beyond the maple tree at the shoreline. She walked over to the back kitchen window and leaned over to see out under the cafe curtains. A black sky in the north was looming over the trees. "There's a storm a coming," she said to the empty room. Large drops of water started falling in the backyard and before she could straighten up, the bottom fell out of the sky. She hurried though the house closing windows and her thoughts returned to Harry. Lightning crashed and lit up the evening sky. It was not chain lightning, but a brush stroke of yellow and orange against the cloud and fog filled sky. The roar of thunder quickly followed it. Worry overtook her and occupied her thoughts. She found herself standing in front of the stove, absentmindedly preparing a cup of orange pekoe tea to calm her nerves. She was taking a cup out of the cabinet when the voice of the storm rang out again and shook the house and causing her to drop her cup. It bounced off the counter and crashed onto the floor. She had taken the broom and dustpan out of the cellar stairway when she heard a car pull up. "He's home," she said hopefully, yet knowing full well that it was not yet time for him to leave college.

She went out on the porch and saw a pencil thin man thrusting an umbrella out of his car and sliding himself underneath it. He walked under the protection of his umbrella the three steps it took him to get from car to porch. Protecting the pinstriped suit that Adele assumed consisted of less material than the umbrella guarding it, he backed up the steps. He closed his umbrella, shook the rain off of it, rolled it and fastened the enclosure. He shook it again and hooked it over the bend of his arm. He then removed the bowler he was wearing, shook the water off of it, and replaced it on his head and with a peculiar swiping motion adjusting it to his satisfaction. He straightened his tie and tugged at the hem of his suit coat. Finally, he rotated to make his introduction. The entire process took so long that Adele almost went back inside to sweep up the shattered remains of her cup. She was sure she would be back on the porch before he completed his grooming.

"I hope I am at the proper address," he squeaked. "I am in search of Mrs. Harry Wallace of Jonasport, formerly Adele Susannah Abbott of Gray Island."

"You're at the right house. I am Adele Wallace."

"Splendid," he proclaimed. He whipped a business card from a wallet in his inner jacket pocket. The motion was so smooth that Adele imagined him practicing it in front of a mirror as a young boy practiced the quick draw of his western hero with a cap pistol. "Mrs. Wallace", he held the card and made his introduction without pause or forethought "Timothy P. Smiley, Oakhurst and Smiley, attorneys at law, at your service." She had met Oakhurst at the reading of Albert's will. She always wondered what a lawyer named Smiley would look like. Now she knew. "I have been in a desperate search for you. It began with a request from colleagues in Bowdenville. They began their search with the records from the Ebeneezer Baptist Church, where you attended some Sunday school classes. From there they spoke to the former harbormaster who recalled that your mother (May God rest her soul) and you traveled to our fair county to work at the now defunct sardine factory. Well, I took it from there; employee records, school records, some very vague town reports, they don't keep very proper records down here. Let me tell you it was exhausting, but here I am and here you are."

"Mr. Smiley," Adele replied in exasperation. "What can I do for you?" Lawyer Smiley was disappointed that she failed to share his enthusiasm or appreciate his hard work.

"Mrs. Wallace, your father is dead."

When Harry got home Adele was sitting in her room looking at a picture she had pulled out of her old family Bible. He called to her twice and, when she didn't answer, he went upstairs to find her. He sat next to her on his great-grandmother's bed.

"Who's that?"

"It's my Papa." She went on to explain the visit from lawyer Smiley. Her Papa had been living in the old house since the day after Adele and her mother crossed the river. He made no attempt to find them. With his death, the home she escaped from was now hers.

"What are you going to do with it?"

"I don't know. Sell it, I guess. I don't want it."

"Whatever you think is best. I tell you what. Tomorrow is Saturday. Let's go take a look at it and you can decide from there…. if you're up to it." His maturity surprised her and swelled her heart. She kissed his cheek.

"I'm up to it."

That night Adele had a fitful sleep. In her dreams she saw her mother standing in the middle of Penobscot Bay. She was wearing a tight red dress shimmering in the sun. Its hem stopped at mid-thigh. Her hair was bobbed with spit curls plastered around the outline of her face. She wore a pearl necklace that was longer than her dress. It was tied in a knot at her breast. Her face was painted with make-up and her lips were ruby red. She smoked a cigarette attached to a long holder. She held a champagne glass in her hand and was waving it at little Adele, encouraging her to come join her. Little Adele got up off the large rock she was sitting on and started out to her when someone grabbed her from behind. She tried to escape, her arms flailing and reaching out to her mother. She looked up to see who was holding her and saw the face of Albert Pritchard. He didn't look at her, but stared off to the other shore, his face set and determined. Little Adele turned back to call out to her mother, but she was gone. In her stead was the grim reaper. He turned in disappointment and slowly sank into the water below him.

Harry's night was not much better than his mother's, although dreamless. He lay awake worrying about his mother. When he finally did get to sleep, it was but a brief rest. He awoke early, determined not to let his mother go to Gray Island. He would go see the house alone, determine the value, and put it up for sale. She was already awake and dressed when he came downstairs. He pitched his proposal and she declined the offer. He insisted and she resisted. Finally, in exasperation, he blurted out. "I'm only looking out for your best interest. I should think you would see that. I should think you would listen to me, Ma. I should think you would appreciate it." She looked at him calmly but sternly. He shivered.

"My dear Harry, if you wish to be seen, you should stand up. If you wish to be heard, you should speak up. But if you wish to be appreciated, you should shut up. Now get dressed. We'll take your car."

As they crossed the bridge on to the island, Adele told Harry to stop at the Gray Town Hall. "I need to pay the back taxes."

"Back taxes, how much?"

She turned to him with raised eyebrows. "Are you paying them?"

"But Ma, we don't even know its worth. It could be less than the tax bill!"

"Its worth has nothing to do with it. It's owed. And now I owe it. I'll not have my name in the Gray Town Report for nonpayment of taxes."

"But…" Adele raised a gloved hand. Harry fell silent and pulled alongside the sidewalk in front of the Gray Island Town Hall.

"Harry, some of the tax will go to feed the poor children of this island. You'll understand well enough when you see them."

Adele closed her eyes as they descended Hardscrabble Hill. She didn't want to see. Harry, on the other hand, was taking it all in. He started inspecting the houses as soon as they reached the island. He was trying to draw conclusions about what was to come from the environment. Some of the houses were really nice. It might not be that bad. He would soon discover that it was that bad, and worse. The further down the road they traveled, the worse the condition of it got. The houses along side of the road followed the same pattern. Adele opened her eyes. "It's coming up", she quietly stated. She pointed to the left and Harry pulled into the yard of the house his mother used to call home. Harry wanted to close *his* eyes.

The roof of the outhouse, he assumed it was the outhouse, had caved in. A fallen birch tree had landed on top of it. The door was opened and hung cockeyed. One of its hinges had pulled loose. One wall of the shed had caved in, dropping the roof and converting the structure to a lean-to. The house was intact, but not one drop of paint had ever touched its walls. It was smaller than the garage Tommy had built to store Harry's and his mother's cars.

Adele got out and walked towards the house, but then turned and walked down an overgrown path that led to the water. She brushed alder branches aside as she went. Harry stayed behind gawking in disbelief at the house. He could not believe that his mother ever lived in such a dismal place. After a few minutes he followed the path his mother had taken. She was at the shoreline, sitting on a small rock. The hem of her dress was lying in the wet sand and seaweed the tide had left behind. She was looking at their house across the bay. When he knelt next to her, she patted his leg twice and said, "Well." He helped her up and she walked back up the path to confront her childhood. As they opened the door to the house, a wharf rat ran out over her foot.

"Jesus," Harry cried out. Adele did not flinch.

"Don't blame Him," she advised. Spiders and rats had redecorated the house. Empty liquor bottles were as abundant as the rocks on the shore. The place was devoid of linen, no curtains on the windows, no sheets on the bed, and no clothes or towels were to be found. A path was beaten into the dust and dirt that led from the door to the kitchen table, through the bedroom door, and ending at the bed. Ancient and recent vomit stains covered the path and bed. Harry evoked the name of the Son of God three more times before Adele exited the house and went to the car. She never uttered a word.

When Harry started the car and pulled away he asked, "What do you want to do with it?"

Adele never looked back, but stared up Hardscrabble Hill. She quietly answered her son. "Let the rats have it."

Chapter Twenty-eight

An uneventful winter came and went. Harry commuted back and forth to college. Adele traveled back and forth to Colcord's store, her meetings at the Woman's Auxiliary, (where she now presided as president), and the homes of friends. Tommy hurried back and forth from his businesses to the bank, and called Adele and Harry on the weekends. Spring came and went in the same manner. But when summer came Adele and Harry's routine changed, while Tommy's remained the same. Mother and son spent many hours on the porch and in the sitting room playing chess and listening to radio programs. They walked on the shore where Adele would listen to Harry's big plans for the future. They frequented Little Jeff's ice cream parlor for hot fudge sundaes, Sarah's Diner for clam baskets, and, on Wednesday night, they had a sit-down supper at Reed's Restaurant. They went once a week to Beano and on Sunday they went to church together. At night Harry went out with his friends or his girlfriend of the week. Adele sat in her Queen Anne chair and soaked her aching feet, secretly wishing September would come. When it did come she wished it had not.

But as the earth never stops turning, the seasons continue to change. September arrived and departed and arrived and departed again.

One day when Harry was in his junior year of college, Adele was looking out her bedroom window remembering the beautiful yellow, brown, and orange of the fall foliage, and marveling at the cleansing white of the snow that had again fallen on New England. She was so intent in her wonder that she failed to hear the old truck that pulled up into the drive. She did, however, hear the pounding on the back door and went downstairs to answer the pounding.

An old man dressed in overalls and wearing a barn coat stood at her door. He clutched a rabbit fur hat in his hands. Adele opened the door and pushed open the screen door.

"Is the good doctor available?" He asked politely.

"Dr. Pritchard passed away some years back."

"Great," a voice to her lower right said. Adele looked down and saw a teenage girl sitting on the floor of the porch, leaning against the outside wall of the house. A cloth valise lay at her feet.

"That's gonna be a problem," the ancient farmer said. Adele looked at the emptiness in his eyes. She noticed the wrinkles the years had left on his brow, but an absence of smile lines around his temples.

"Pardon me?"

"Madam, Satan has visited my home. He left his seed in my great-granddaughter here." He pointed to the girl. "Just like her mother and her mother before her, she is a curse on my life. I have prayed all night about my plight and the Lord directed me here. The doctor removed the bastard child of her sinful mother." He started backing up. "It's better that she stay here where sin is abides, than in the home of a God-fearing man." He turned and hurried off the porch and into his truck. Adele thought to call after him, but she was too stunned to speak. She silently watched him pull off.

The voice to the lower right informed her, "He always talks like that." Adele turned and looked at her with mouth agape. The abandoned girl purposely did not look at Adele, choosing instead to stare at the garage doors. "So, are you gonna help me?"

"I'm going to try," Adele said, still in shock.

"You gonna help me abort this baby?"

The shock wore off. "I certainly am not."

"Great!"

Adele began to get a little angry. "How old are you?"

The impudent girl drew her head back, and then threw it forward launching the words at Adele. "…Twenty-one!"

Adele opened the screen door and holding it open, she pushed the back door open in an act of invitation. "So, you're a fool *and* a liar." Knowing she had been pegged, the girl rose, snatched up her valise, and went into the dining room. Adele followed her in and closed the door. "Follow me," she instructed and led her guest upstairs and into Isabelle's room.

The girl glanced around at the old, frilly furnishings that made up the room. "Jesus Christ, what old crow lived in here?" Adele thought, *Isabelle Pritchard,* but she said, "Would you prefer to stay in the cellar?"

"No."

"No, ma'am.", Adele corrected.

"No, ma'am," she spat.

"Then you will refrain from criticizing my home or the furnishings in it. Is that understood?"

Sarcasm was her weapon. "Yes MA'AM!" She drew out the ma'am for emphasis.

Adele reached down inside of her and pulled out Nurse Abbott. She glared down at the girl. "Listen carefully, for I shall not repeat myself. You have but two choices. One, you can stay in my house until accommodations can be made that are more suitable to you *and* to me. Two, I can go down and telephone Sheriff Poulin who will escort your down to the home for unwed mothers in Augusta. Make your decision now!"

The girl's survival instinct took over and her attitude changed immediately. Her face softened, the hardness in her body relaxed, and her head dropped. "I'd rather stay here.... ma'am."

Adele put Nurse Abbott away for now. "You don't have to say it at the end of every sentence." She pulled open an empty drawer of the bureau. "You can put your things in here. I'll draw you a nice bath. You smell of smoke. Then, we'll have some supper." She started to leave. "Oh, what is your name?"

The girl was opening her valise. "Rebecca Storm. My friends call me Becky."

"Well, Becky. I'm Adele. Welcome to my home."

"Thank you ma'am," Becky answered as she placed her unwashed clothes in the drawer.

When Harry returned from school, Adele and Becky were sitting at the kitchen table eating corned beef hash. Adele had prepared a New England boiled dinner the night before, and she and Harry had enjoyed it in the dining room. But corned beef hash is better digested in the kitchen. Adele made the formal introductions and Harry loaded a plate with hash and sat at the table to eat. He looked up at Becky between bites. When supper was over, he asked to be excused and retired to the sitting room to read his college text. Becky offered to help Adele with the dishes, but Adele declined. She felt the girl had been through a difficult day and should try to relax. There would be time enough for chores tomorrow. Becky followed Harry's lead and asked to be excused, something she had never heard done before. Adele nodded and Becky took the path she had seen Harry take. She sat in the Queen Anne chair and gazed at the fire. Harry started to tell her that was his mother's place in the sitting room, but held his tongue. He waited with baited breath for Adele to come in and roust her from it. He wanted to witness the expression on her face and possible argument that might ensue. Adele put away the last plate and joined the young people. When she sat in the less comfortable Louis XIV, Harry got up dejected and went to his room to continue his studies.

Alone by the fire, the females talked. Adele gave Becky a brief and general history of her life. Becky returned with her own story, but her telling included the details which led up to her present condition. She had met a merchant sailor and they fell in love. He was different from the local boys she had been out with and had promised that one day they would get married. But when she got pregnant, he asked her how he could be sure that he was the father. Becky had known other men, and everyone in town knew it. She swore to him that it was his child. Then, he told her that he would support the child, but no port was his home and he wouldn't marry her. He boarded the next ship out and left her with a baby in her womb and a broken heart. She did not know the whereabouts of her mother or the identity of her father. Her grandmother was in the woman's prison for stabbing a carnival worker, and her great-grandparents were her final hope. But they didn't want her.

This story was told in two locations. The part about her condition was told where Harry had left them. Hearing mention of a merchant marine brought painful memories to Adele, who decided to drown them in a cup of tea. The story of Becky's sordid genealogy was told at the kitchen stove. Harry heard them in the kitchen and went back downstairs to eavesdrop from the sitting room. When the tea was ready Becky took hers up to her new bedroom and Adele took hers to the sitting room. Harry was sitting in her chair. She gave him the look every mother gives and every offspring knows. He got up and she set her tea on the side table, smoothed her dress, and sat down. Harry, completely dissatisfied with how the evening had gone, decided to end it. "Good night, ma."

"Harry, before you go, could you throw a piece of wood on the fire?" Harry tossed a stick on the grate. "And tell your mother what has put a bee in your britches?"

Harry turned to face his mother. "Ma, we have to talk."

"So talk."

He knew he could solve this problem with one sentence, although he didn't want to say it. But drastic times call for drastic measures. He knew she meant well, but sometimes she went overboard. He peeked up the stairs from around the corner of the wall and closed the door. The action disturbed her. He sat on the sofa. "Ma, I've seen her at Clancy's."

"…And?" He was stunned.

"MA….Clancy's…The roadhouse; you know what I'm saying."

"I believe I do." She was nodding her head. Harry felt some relief. "You've seen Rebecca at the bar that you frequent. And you assume that makes her unfit to be in my home, whereas it's okay for you to be here." His relief had a short life. "So, did you talk to her there?"

"Well, yes, I've talked to her. She was going out with Dickie Partridge."

"But you don't choose to speak with her here."

"Ma, I'm a man. It's different for me to be there. No, wait. I mean…."

"You mean there are two kinds of women; one you bring home to Momma and one you bring home when Momma is not there?"

"Ma, you're putting words in my mouth."

"Well, allow me to put a few in your ear. I certainly don't approve of the path that young lady has chosen for herself. But she has no less right to walk into an establishment of that nature than you. Possession of a penis does not empower you to do anything a woman cannot; except to pee standing up. It does not give you the right to judge that girl unless you are willing to stand in judgment of yourself. Now, your prejudice has upset me enough for one night. Good night." She rose and left him there to ponder what she had said. The next morning he greeted their house-guest with a more tolerate attitude. He never visited Clancy's again.

Becky stayed with them for two months. Adele was hoping that life in the two-story colonial would be a positive influence on her. Harry had

212

almost begun to like her. One early morning Harry went to the garage to get a book he hoped he had left in his car. Adele was sitting at the kitchen table reading that morning's edition of the *Soctomah Crier* when he raced back into the house and tore up the stairs. "Our home is not a racetrack, Harry." *Some things change, some things never change.* Harry stepped quietly into the kitchen. *That's better.* She was reading an article about the stalemate at the 38th parallel. "I said last June when that fool president let McArthur invade Puson that it was a mistake. Now look at the mess we're in."

"Ma", Harry calmly called.

"Harry, never trust a man who clenches a pipe in his teeth. He's only trying to bite his tongue."

"Becky's gone."

Adele put her paper down and exhaled. "That stupid, stupid girl…. this was her chance. Why would she not take it?"

"She stole my car, Ma." Adele sprang from her chair and began to pace the room. She stopped, raced into the den, and took her purse out of her handbag. Harry was on her heels when she opened it. Adele dropped her head.

"Damn, damn, damn…" Harry went to the den and dialed the sheriff. After giving the dispatcher the description of the girl and the car, he searched for and found his mother sitting on the icy steps at the shore. "Your momma is an old fool."

"My momma is a kind and caring woman. You're still a nurse. You help people. Ma, it's easy to be good to average people. It takes someone special to reach out to people like Becky." He gently helped her up and escorted her to the warmth of the house.

The next day Sheriff Poulin drove into the yard. One of his deputies was following in Harry's car. The sheriff told Adele the girl had no money on her when they found her. Adele had her doubts, but was happy to get the car back. He related that Becky was found on Route One near the New Hampshire border. They had taken her to the hospital instead of jail. She told them she rolled the car out into the street and started it after it coasted around horny corner. The strain caused her to hemorrhage. She was on her way to New York to find the father of her unborn child. Her actions failed to gain her a husband, and had caused her to lose her child, and her freedom.

Harry refrained from saying the four words that all people who are wrong dread hearing. As Adele climbed the stairs that night, she thanked him for his restraint.

Sleep brought her another dream. This time it was Becky attempting to free herself from a captor at the shore. And though she didn't see the face, Adele knew she was the one trying to hold the girl back. She failed, and mercifully awoke before she learned whether the girl had sunk or swam. Perhaps if she had given Becky more details in the story she told her, if she had been a little more forthcoming about her past and how she escaped it, the outcome would have been different. She switched on her bedside lamp and looked to a rectangle of wallpaper brighter than the rest of the paper on the wall. She was looking at the spot where the picture she gave Tommy once hung. Then she switched the room back into darkness. Her dark secrets still haunted her.

Chapter Twenty-nine

The year after Becky lost her last chance for a decent life, Harry graduated from college with a bachelor's degree in agricultural science. He planned to take over the potato acreage in Scotia County. He had some theories about fertilization and was anxious to try them out. But, he never got the chance.

One week after graduation he was drafted into the armed forces. Because of his college degree, he received an officer's commission. After a training period on surviving war, which was half as short as the safety training he received at Avery and Sons, he was sent to Korea to serve as an adjutant to a brass-laden general who was supposed to be leading the 4th Infantry Division in Operation Counter, another one of McArthur's failed attempt to squash the red menace. En route to pick up some smoked heron for his general, Harry's jeep tire rolled over a land mine. The general was devastated by the loss and sent another junior office to procure some more heron. The army sent Harry's body home in a pine box.

Tommy flew back to Maine on the day Adele called him. He found her in bed. She stayed there until the funeral. Tommy signed for Harry's body at the train depot and it was sent by hearse to Jenkins and Smith. He fed Adele in her bed, and sat by her each night until she fell asleep. On the day before the funeral he was in the den making a phone call to his office in Massachusetts. After some heated discussion with one of his assistants, Tommy hollered into the receiver, "I told you I don't know when or if I'll be back!" Adele heard this from her bed. She got up, donned her robe, and went downstairs. She began to revisit the memories in her home. From the foyer she peered into the sitting room and saw Albert lying on the sofa kicking the afghan off his legs. She walked into the dining room and saw Tommy and his boys enjoying their first meal in a room dedicated for that purpose. In the kitchen she saw little Harry hiding under Millie's dress. She entered the den and touched Tommy on the shoulder. "Okay then", he said to the receiver. "If you can handle things, I may stay in a little longer". He looked up and smiled at Adele.

"Mr. Avery", said the voice in the telephone. "I don't know what…" Tommy ignored the plea running through the wires.

"Its sounds like a fine plan. I'll call you later in the week." Adele did not hear the conversation Tommy invented for her comfort. She was viewing in her mind a younger version of herself taking a book off the shelf and replacing it with the one she had just read. Tommy hung up the phone as she was scanning the titles of Albert's books. "Oh, good, you're up. That's good Adele. Can I get you some tea?'

216

"Call him back, Tommy."

"What do you mean…?"

She turned to him and took his hands. "Your life is in Massachusetts. My life, or what is left of it, is in this house. I know what you're trying to do, but you have worked too hard to give it all up and just to go back to square one."

"I love you, Adele. And you need me"

"Then go home, Tommy. Go home so you will continue to love me and not grow to resent me. That is what I need you to do"

Adele buried her son in the plot purchased for her, between his father and his Bumper. His mortal coil would spend an eternity beneath a sunny slope on bank of the Penobscot River. Abner Thomas presided over the funeral in his wheelchair. Adele and Tommy wrote the eulogy. Post 157 of the American Legion played taps and marked his grave with the legion emblem and a small American flag.

After the service Tommy returned to Massachusetts and Adele returned to her white two-story colonial. And, as much as she wanted to, she didn't die. She lived for three more decades and wore out two rockers. She crocheted mounds of Afghans, which ended up permeating not only the town of Jonasport, but also the surrounding towns of Soctomah County. When the word got out people would come to buy them from her, not because they wanted one, but because they wanted to sit on her porch and listen to her tell them of stories of old Maine, when neighbors were friends and community mattered.

The summer of 1982 found the residents of Maine recovering from a brutal winter. Tommy had come from Massachusetts to open the storms windows of Adele's home, and add a fresh coat of white paint to the porch. He painted the floor and steps forest green, and had added sand to the paint of the steps to prevent Adele from slipping on them and falling to the ground. He feared the worst, should such a fall occur. As he was boarding a plane to go home (His advancing years prevented him from taking the trip in his car), she stepped out to her porch with a glass of cold water that she poured from a plastic milk jug she kept in the refrigerator. She sat it on her little, white wrought-iron table. She went back into the house and got an orange, a paper towel and a paring knife with a chipped bone handle and a broken tip. These she placed on the table along side of her glass of water. She wrapped an afghan around her legs and pulled a silk scarf from the front pocket of her house dress and tied it in her hair to keep the wind from destroying her hairdo. Now prepared to meet the day, she peeled her orange and took in the view that she never tired of seeing. Across the bay, on the other shore, she spied what she thought was a little girl sitting on a rock on the shore of Gray Island. The little girl was looking at her house. Adele rose, crossed the porch, and leaned against the railing to get a better look. Squint as she might, she could not focus. Determined, she went in the house to get the field glasses that Tommy had bought her to watch the eagles soaring above and the loons nesting below. She looked across with the glasses and the little girl was gone. She searched up and down the shoreline of Gray Island, but to no avail. Assigning it to a foolish old woman's imagination, she sat back in her rocker and ate her orange, glancing up from time to time, just in case.

That night, as she slept, the *Sovereign State* sailed into her dreams. When the gangplank was lowered, Adele Susannah Abbott Wallace boarded her and sailed away.

Chapter Thirty

Thomas Avery sat on the porch of the home of his good friend. How many times had he sat here before? He took in the picture before him. The blue and silver rippling of the bay waters; the billowing white clouds (cumulus, he thought) floating, drifting across a bright blue sky; the light green trees of the island across the water, turning a dark green as the clouds pass over them; bits of white of houses against the green, and of sailboats against the blue; one solitary speck of green, almost fluorescent, bobbing stationary in the bay, marking the port side of the channel. He saw in his mind the red buoy marking the starboard side, but his eyes couldn't see it behind the massive maple tree on the shore, planted there years back to protect the house from the fierce wind that comes with a nor'easter. He saw sea ducks gathered in the cove and seagulls soaring above. He saw the seaweed on the flats disappear slowly as the tide flowed in. He noticed the movement of an aluminum boat buoyed off the shore; a boat that he knew was set down solidly in the mud when he came out to sit.

My god, how long had he been sitting here? He looked at his watch and sighed.

"Well", he said quietly. "It's time."

He rose and walked into the house. The idyllic image he tried to relax with was quickly replaced with the dread of what was to come. The creaking of the screen door evoked a warm memory that he pushed from his mind. On the plane from Boston, he formulated a plan for survival. He would do this, but he would do it mechanically; no feeling, no memories, do it and go. Therefore, disciplined, he walked quickly to the stairs, dodging the table, refusing to look at the room, and, thus, depriving his mind of years of memories built around the dining room table.

Up the stairs and into the bathroom, he turned on the shower and disrobed. He stayed in longer than usual, hoping the steaming mist would wash away more that the day's dirt and perspiration. Then, toweling off, he walked into the doctor's room, where he put his suitcase the night before. He had quietly shut the doors of two of the three remaining bedrooms with the old and newer beds, respectively, knowing he could not enter either.

He removed his clothing choice for this occasion from a Brooks Brothers suit bag and laid it on the bed; black, single-breasted coat, pants with no cuff. He choose a gray Van Heusen shirt with white cuffs and collar, black Florsheim's and a black tie that he laced in front of the dresser mirror (he could never tie one without looking at it), and then, donning his jacket, he was ready.

He was halfway down the staircase when he noticed the Persian runner with the brass stair rods holding it in place. He could almost hear her say, "A dollar and fifteen cents apiece for eleven steps? That's highway robbery!" And after later finding the cheap imitations in the Sears & Roebuck catalog, "Three dollars for the whole set. Who's gonna know the difference?" He noted that she was right. After fifty years she had never been found out.

He climbed slowly back up, went down the hall and opened the door to her bedroom. The smell of White Shoulders seemed to still fill the air. He walked to the corner of the room and stared at an 8x10 rectangle on the wall, a brighter patch of wallpaper standing out against the faded paper of the rest of the room. He turned and exited and found himself at the door of Newer Bed's room. His hand reached out, but stopped, trembling at the knob. He drew it back as though he had been burned, did an about face and hurried from the house to his rental car. He was on his way to Jenkins & Smith funeral home, and he prayed for the strength to carry him through.

He walked to his rental car after the service and heard his name called. He turned and, seeing no one he knew, continued on his way.

"Sir, oh sir, could I have a moment of your time!" He turned to face an overweight stranger. He was wearing a golf shirt and short pants. He was out of breath. Between gasps he said, "I understand she left you the house."

"Do I know you?" The stranger thrust a card into the mourner's hand. As he read the card, the pitch continued.

"Eric Stall, Stall Realtors and Associates, sir, I can get you a nice price for that house. I have sold three homes in that town this month."

The card was handed back to the realtor. When he did not accept it, it was dropped to the ground. "The house is not for sale." The out of shape realtor grunted as he bent over to retrieve his card from the ground.

"Oh, you're going to reside there? Well, if you ever decide..."

"The property is being deeded to the State of Maine." The mourner unlocked the car and Mr. Stall leaned in against the door.

"You're giving it away. Sir, we're taking about a valuable piece of property. People are dying to get a hold of an authentic sea captains house. You can't be serious."

The perspective prey shoved the round little man off his car door. "That is not a piece of property, you vulture. It is the home of Adele Wallace and her son Harry. No man will ever reside in it again...now good day!"

The following day Tommy traveled to the state capital in Augusta and signed the necessary paperwork to ensure that Adele's house would become a legacy to the woman who climbed Hardscrabble Hill and, once at the top devoted her life to the service of those around her. The house and property, as well as the land across the bay on Gray Island, was signed over to the state and are now part of the State of Maine Park system. Adele had always told him that she wished that all the children of Maine would have a place to sit on the shore and dream of their future.

He took a Delta flight to Boston and was picked up at the airport by his chauffeur. He arrived at his home thirty minutes later. As he walked through the door, his housekeeper took his suitcase and asked, "Difficult trip, sir?"

"Yes", he said, "very."

"Shall I prepare you something to eat, sir?"

"No…. thank you, I'm good."

He opened the twin doors of his study and closed them behind him. By the glow of the fireplace, he inspected an 8x10 illustration cut from a magazine. He saw the tack hole that once secured it to a stud of a cabin. Its 12x15 mahogany frame now held it behind an acid free mat to preserve it for the remainder of his life. Reaching up he touched its caption. He backed up and sat in his overstuffed leather chair. Thinking that he was alone, he dropped his head into his hands.

A little boy put his arm around a little girl of equal height and age and whispered into her ear, "Mr. Avery is crying."

The End